KILTS AND HIDDEN CRUSHES

Café owner Callie Dewar finds the return of her teenage crush too hot to handle. Hamish Gordon is back in St. Andrews, volunteering as a waiter while secretly yearning to rekindle the spark that's been smouldering between them. The pair are unwittingly brought together for a holiday in the Highlands — but Callie is harbouring a deep secret that she dare not share with anyone, least of all Hamish. Will she succeed in pushing her hunky ex-flame away? Or will kilted chemistry, family trickery, and an errant sheep change their destinies?

JUDY JARVIE

KILTS AND HIDDEN CRUSHES

Complete and Unabridged

LINFORD
Leicester

First published in Great Britain in 2016

First Linford Edition
published 2017

A catalogue record for this book is available
from the British Library.

ISBN 978–1–4448–3400–0

Published by
F. A. Thorpe (Publishing)
Anstey, Leicestershire

Set by Words & Graphics Ltd.
Anstey, Leicestershire
Printed and bound in Great Britain by
T. J. International Ltd., Padstow, Cornwall

This book is printed on acid-free paper

1

'Those lads have fine, strong legs and muscles.'

'Have you seen the big one's smile?'

'With a voice like warmed heather honey. Best thing to happen here for years. I pass three times a day to peek through the window.'

'And I'm overindulging on Callie's cupcakes. It's playing havoc with my waistline and my purse, but the view's worth the calories. He can butter my scones any day.'

Callie Dewar heard her customers' comments, but they didn't stop her from wanting to give Hamish Gordon his marching orders. Her fledgling business, The Caledonian Cupcake Café, had women flocking, panting like lust-fuelled lunatics. Queues lined the street outside most days. All because she'd established kilted waiters as her unique sales ploy. But she never should have listened to Linley, her best friend who was also Hamish's sister. What had she been thinking?

Callie pushed through the kitchen opening, skidding to a halt before her nemesis. 'I need table four. Would you mind dropping off their bill? Or haven't you finished flirting yet?'

Inside her, a tiny gremlin voice nagged that she always came out armed for warfare with Hamish, and maybe she needed to ease up. But that was what he got for being too good-looking, with a flirtation black belt and an inborn ability to bait her to crazy point.

'Easy there, Callie. Whoa, take a slow breath,' Hamish answered. And her heart sped in her chest because he somehow set it to aerobic-mode.

'I don't need breathing tuition. I need you to clear tables faster.'

Everything about him riled her. The hint of dark stubble that so became him. The biceps kissed by his T-shirt's sleeves. The way his eyes danced when he made fun of her. All of that in triplicate, with a 'Stay Back — Toxic — Danger' sign to boot.

His strong hands steadied Callie, and her heart thumped under his quizzical stare. She wished she didn't have such a startling response to his touch. She also wished he didn't make her tongue go dry. And she hated that she had no control over her reactions — as much as she hated having him in her café. Joking. Showing off his charms. Why couldn't he have stayed in Strasbourg, where he belonged?

'You telling me we should be chasing our customers away now, Callie?' His Scots brogue was yet another asset.

Answer to his question: yes. She did want the customers gone. And him with them. Especially when they were blonde with long, curly eyelashes that batted non-stop. And when she had to hear their flirty laughter drifting towards her kitchen. But she couldn't admit jealous vibes. Not to anyone. Especially not herself.

'I'm concerned that our table turn-around's dragging,' she said. 'If you don't mind, just move them on.'

'You're too strict.'

'I'm also the boss. Or had you forgotten that again?'

'Forget? You never let me.' His almost hidden smile made her antsy. 'The customer at four is an old school friend. I promise I'll do better. She's done nothing but compliment your baking, but I'll enforce her exit without further ado.' To screw the punch, he saluted her, and that made her itch to lash out again. She buried the urge deep.

Hamish wore his family heirloom sporran with a khaki and beige kilt. A white T-shirt hugged his chest, while big boots underlined the rebel vibe. And he looked way too good in it all. His spiced cologne teased Callie's nostrils, and the fact she liked it annoyed her more.

'Get reacquainted in your own time,' she told him. 'I'm sure you can charm her into moving to permit space.'

His gaze stayed on her, probing, so she turned away. Why did she react so? But she knew the answer: a teenage

4

crush that had caused a dented ego (hers), and a hurt that had lingered even after a decade's avoidance. The end result was petty spats like this one. It annoyed her as much as the fact that she still cared.

'Callie, are you having a bad day?' Hamish's gaze speared hers when she chanced a glance. She couldn't help but notice his fine grey eyes and hair lightly dusted with the first specks of steel-grey.

'I was doing fine until service started to crawl,' she said. 'There's a business association networking event tonight. I've agreed to cater, which means I'm up to my neck, and I've been flat out all day.'

'FYI, I'm not flirting. I only aim to keep your customers happy.' Hamish flexed his jaw and pivoted. 'But point taken. Though I think you could do with some chill factor in the cake mix, boss.'

Callie longed to accuse him of flirting with all the women in the place. Words failed her primarily because customers sat nearby; ones who'd take it all in gladly and telegraph it around the place. She swallowed her urge with a chaser of chagrin.

While Hamish went back to his admirers, Callie returned to the kitchen, where two dozen choux pastries awaited icing. But her present mood could sour eclairs with a glance.

St. Andrews, in Scotland's kingdom of Fife, was a tiny but bustling cosmopolitan coastal city famed for its pro golf, its university, and for being where Prince William fell for his Princess, Katherine. Now it had a new prince, and she'd have banished Hamish, but he'd arrived when she'd been desperately under-resourced.

'Okay there, Cal?' Jonty asked. An inquisition by her sous-chef was the last thing she needed as a curtain-call. 'You're staring at those cupcakes like you're about to detonate them or sling them at the wall. Should I run for cover?' Jonty Baird's wild red dreadlocks were stuffed into a Scots Saltire flag bandana.

'I'll be glad when this lot is delivered safely to the business association. We're nearly done, thank goodness. Then I have paperwork to tackle after the meeting. Going to be a long day. Is it me, or is Hamish a mega-flirt who pushes all my buttons?'

'No comment. You know what they say — if you've got it, flaunt it . . . and he's got plenty. Man in a skirt, girls want to flirt. Your brainwave to introduce kilts really was a moment of genius.' Jonty licked her tasting spoon and then her lips for emphasis. 'What d'ya reckon? Is Hamish St. Andrews's most wanted man? Should we organise a poll?' She waggled her eyebrows.

'I'll pass.'

'You sure?'

Deep down Callie knew she needed a good, long break. From the café, full stop. And from a life that wasn't turning out as she'd hoped. As an afterthought she added, 'You're married. You shouldn't be noticing other men.'

'I'm only spectating. Hamish is too

7

easy on them to not take note. Anyway, you can deny all you like, but our top waiter is blessed with charms that make women wish.'

'Wish to escape.' Callie chewed her lip. 'Waving his confidence in my face. D'you think I'm uptight?'

Why was she asking Jonty? Jonty wasn't privy to the knowledge that Hamish had been the object of Callie's fruitless crush for way too long. Or that when she'd finally got courage a decade before and admitted her attraction, he'd dashed her hopes with a U-turn. Right at the moment she'd fallen into his embrace — only it turned out it was a pity one. So she'd got it wrong. Nice ego slice. Was it any wonder she found him hard to take?

Jonty stared like a fish scooped from the pond by a cat's paw. She opted for leap and retreat, and Callie watched in shock as Jonty darted up the kitchen's deep end. 'Think I need to check my quiches. Don't want scorched savouries, do we?'

At the serving hatch, Callie glimpsed Hamish exchanging numbers with a blonde. A leggy brunette gushed as he passed her too, and Callie saw the look he flashed her.

'Boss, your icing is dripping on your shoes . . . and down your front.' Jonty's voice snatched her back to the present.

Hamish had outstayed his waiting welcome. And it was affecting her ability to stand being in the café at all. She'd have to take action. She laid the bag down and wiped her hands. 'Look; thirty minutes to closing, but I skipped lunch and need a break. You okay keeping an eye and making sure Hamish knuckles down for me? I'll package this lot when I get back.'

'Sure. And no need. I'll do it,' Jonty said, nodding. 'You look beat. I can handle getting the food into the delivery van when it gets here. Relax and get ready. Just don't wind up in the Auld Hoose Tavern, drinking to Hamish's demise. I don't want you missing tonight's meeting when it's your chance to shine.' Jonty didn't realise just how much Callie did need a break. And ideally much longer than an hour's respite.

'Excuse me, waiter?' a newly arrived redhead shouted to Hamish, and Callie and Jonty clocked her advances. 'You open to offers of dinner, and what time do you finish?' Half the café clientele laughed. The other half wished they'd got in first.

Callie untied and balled her apron and grabbed her keys. Under her breath she whispered, 'Hamish Gordon has to go! But for now I'm going to blame his meddling, crazy-brained sister.'

★ ★ ★

Hamish watched Callie's denim jacket-clad back leave via the café's backdoor. The door slammed in her wake, and he winced that he hadn't come to ask her to step outside and talk sooner. Damn! They couldn't carry on like this; he wouldn't put either of them through more. He'd tried everything, and nothing worked with Callie. Now he'd missed his window to talk.

Jonty rushed by with a tray of quiches. The aromas of basil and tomato made his stomach growl a welcome. It was closer to teatime than he'd realised, and he'd only managed to half eat a sandwich at lunch.

'Okay there, Hamish?' Jonty checked. 'Want to try a quiche, since your belly growls tell me you need sustenance? I'd be a heartless wretch to deprive you. You counting calories?'

'No thanks, I'm good. Just need a new order pad.' A lie, and not his first. He'd come to speak to Callie, nothing more. And failed.

'Far cupboard next to Callie's desk,' she countered. 'Help yourself.'

Hamish rummaged, trying not to get caught up in the small personal items on Callie's desk area that screamed of her quirks — a bottle of her scent he longed to pocket. A diary with a peacock on the page and recipes noted in her hand. He grabbed the order pad even though it was a total faked task.

He was far from okay. Galaxies from good. But how would he put his predicament into words? *Callie hates me. And it bothers me so much it hurts. How do I get through to her when the only thing that could make her happy is to see me with luggage and a plane ticket?*

He itched to write her his resignation letter right now. But that would leave them even more entrenched in unspoken gripes, and Callie would be understaffed. He knew from Linley how heavy Callie's café burden had become; he'd only agreed to serving because he wanted to help. He didn't mind the break from his usual legal work, but would've preferred Callie to welcome his presence. Instead, everything he did backfired.

Hamish didn't know Jonty that well, and he figured she didn't need a full confessional drama on his stand-off with Callie with half an hour to closing time. 'I'm fine — got the pad. Cheers, Jonty. Great quiches; might buy some for takeout later. My aunt would go crazy over those; might treat her.'

She grinned so hard he felt as if he'd just complimented her most cherished achievements. He appreciated that somebody could still smile at him for real. On sabbatical from a Strasbourg law office that held a gallery of his framed professional awards, Hamish felt unaccountably useless.

'I'll leave a bag with enough for you and your aunt Flora,' Jonty said with a wink. 'You can review the new recipe.'

'Great, will do.' He faked a grin back.

'You and Callie locking horns again?' she asked just as he'd turned to go. 'She's not all bad. Just overworked and trying to keep all the balls in the air. It gets her stressed.'

'She loves me really.' He wished his lie held truth; wished he could prove to her she deserved so much better. But Callie, stubborn as she was work-obsessed, couldn't see past this café. His certificates, compliments and pleading wouldn't win her attention.

He'd lost Callie Dewar for good. And that hurt him more than she'd ever know.

★ ★ ★

Callie pulled on her sun-shades, then raised her face to St. Andrews's evening sun. The breeze off the links and nearby beach that Roger Bannister had made famous in *Chariots of Fire* were a welcome retreat after a day spent in her sticky kitchen.

'What have I done? Except get the help you needed.' Newly wed and returned from honeymoon, Linley Gordon-Melrose batted her lashes and adopted her affronted face.

With a sigh, Callie flopped onto Linley's wicker patio sofa. 'Hamish is driving me nuts. If I'd known he'd be my temp waiter stand-in, I'd have booked a one-way ticket to the Outer Hebrides, for my future spent bell-ringing in a monastery.'

'A prescription for chill pills is all you

need, Cal. Aren't you over-reacting?'

Callie rolled her eyes. 'You sent me him. Find a replacement urgently.' Callie donned her best *take pity on me* face. 'Get Hamish out of my space before I go insane.'

'He can't be that bad.' The breeze whipped Linley's duck-egg chiffon dress and blonde locks. The tan and angelic demeanour belied her devious depths. 'Your summer temp eloped; you needed help, Hamish offered. He's working for no tips and no pay. You two just need your heads banged together.'

'Female customers are drooling. That's not the serious vibe I want.' Callie grasped her chilled lemonade and sipped. 'He flirts non-stop. He's putting more tips in the team jar than I've had hot dinners.'

'Or dates,' Linley muttered. 'Sounds like you're jealous. Maybe you need to get more of a social life yourself.'

Callie wasn't stupid; she knew what Linley had intended by putting Hamish at close range. Now that Linley had bagged her husband in gorgeous pro golfer Carter Melrose, she was up to match-making voodoo. Which was the last thing Callie needed.

Callie put down the glass lest she throw it. 'I'm overworked. And he's over-stepping. I'd rather find someone new.'

'You started the problem when you promised the business association you'd introduce kilted servers to push the tourist trade. Hamish is doing you a favour. Panting customers is good.'

Callie knew her error. The varied cafés and restaurants of St. Andrews had to fight hard for their share of seasonal trade. In fact, 'restaurant' was a dirty word right now; a planning notice had been served indicating a new eatery would be established two doors away. Like they hadn't enough compe-tition. The scale of this development was troubling enough without the Kilted Flirt King buzzing her fraught wires.

She sighed. 'I need to stamp my

position in the marketplace. I'm worried the new place will grab business.'

'People love your high teas. All you need is a break.'

'But this new place couldn't be closer; what if they muscle in? It's bad timing to take time off.'

Callie felt confusion swirl inside her — the quandary swamp sucked her deeper each time she puzzled about what path to take. Maybe she should walk away from the café; maybe that was her out. But Grandpa Angus had toiled to keep his business alive, and the café inheritance brought a hefty guilt after-kick now that she was the one left dragging it with her.

Linley stared hard. 'You're drawing crowds with the kilts. See Hamish as a means to an end. Tourist season is almost over; you'll soon be free. Why not take an earlier break?'

Put like that, Linley made her sound a fuss-pot. But Hamish too ably rocked her rickety fishing boat's ballast. Time to stop the waves and find dry land. 'I can't. And he's overqualified. Why isn't he working as an attorney? Why stay on here after the wedding?' Hamish was a local lad done stellar. He'd gone on to be snapped up for Strasbourg glory in the European Court of Human Rights. It didn't compute, him staying put here.

Linley examined her diamond wedding ring in the sun. 'Says he wants some R and R. Maybe he's just been missing home.'

Callie felt weariness sap her bones; she'd loads to finish before she could stop work tonight. She pressed fingers against her temples. 'I need to get ready for tonight's business bash and go check everything. I'm so tired, Lin. No rest for the wicked.'

Linley added, 'Listen, have you booked a destination for your break yet?'

'Haven't had time — thought I'd go somewhere in the campervan.'

'I'm worried about you. We all are. When was the last time you just enjoyed life?' Her expression told of genuine concern. 'You work way too hard.'

'I'm peddling top speed to stay still. How did life pass me by, Lin?'

Linley sighed. 'Delegate jobs to Hamish; that'll keep him busy. And be kind to yourself, Cal. You still considering selling up, finding a manager?'

'It's not a simple decision to make. Walking away from history and obligations is never easy.' Callie blew out a breath. She itched to ask if Hamish had explained about what had happened with his fiancée. She'd only heard about it secondhand and had been told of a photograph featuring a slim brunette wearing a ring. But she bit back the urge to investigate. He was back with no further talk of his future. She wanted to know but wouldn't push.

Yet Linley was right about her needing a break. If Callie carried on, her dominoes would topple. The family bakery had once skirted closure during her grandfather's time, but rose from the ashes as Callie's café. Though she'd never reached a stage where relaxing was an option. And she doubted Grandpa Angus would approve of her kilted sales tactics, wondering more and more often if it was worth the effort.

She rose. 'You're right. Something has to change, and soon.'

Linley took an envelope from the side of her chair. 'I've taken the liberty of calling the chef we agreed would cover you — he can come on Friday. A gift for you, my super bridesmaid. And because this isn't doing you any good. You need that holiday, so I'm helping you get away.'

Callie threw her a sheepish expression. Inside the envelope was confirmation of café cover. Callie hugged her friend. 'Thanks. I really can't, though; I'm not ready, and Jonty needs me.'

A rose tint covered Linley's cheeks when she replied. 'Actually, she's fine with the plan. I checked it out with her first. She says you need the break. I'm putting things in place.'

'Ganging up, more like.'

Linley stared at her. 'We care about you. You're tired and frazzled; this chef's flying in at Leuchars from catering some celeb bash and he's all set. I'm a millionaire golf pro's wife with my own recruitment company. This time you're taking a proper break of a week or more, and only coming back when you're rested.'

Callie pocketed the envelope. But could she trust a stranger? Could she let go? 'I'll think about it. Gotta go get myself ready for tonight. Love you, Lin.'

As Callie opened the gate, Linley shouted, 'You're going. It's been organised. Don't sack Hamish yet. A chillax is all you need to reset your sense of humour.'

But Callie Dewar had developed a steel backbone in business. So she'd make the decision. And when it came to Hamish, she'd be showing him the door the first chance she got.

2

Callie deeply inhaled the salty tang of the seashore and let the wind's touch ravage her hair. Instead of heading straight to the café to change, she walked on the white sands of St Andrew's beach, stealing a few more minutes of 'life pause'.

Dogs barked, runners pounded, gulls swooped as children played. The beach always provided a busy thoroughfare for a vibrant cosmopolitan local community. Students, academics, golf course glitterati — St. Andrews hosted it all. She should come here more, she decided, enjoying the moment of mindfulness as she selected the driftwood logs and twigs she needed to complete her hobby project. A mirror for Jonty's new sitting-room décor. The sea-blasted glass and pale woods would complement her chosen neutrals theme. In her free time, when Callie had it, interior crafting offered a brain break and creative escape. She loved losing herself in her imagination.

A child's shriek grabbed her attention and made her scan the stretch of sand. She located the tot and recognised the playful action. Callie's heart drummed and her hand shook so much she dropped the wood. No tears. Not here, she told herself.

Laughter followed the screams, dispelling the panic, enforcing the theory that there was actually no problem. No danger risk. But Callie's hands didn't steady.

There were always children here. During the day pre-schoolers toddled with their mothers, and at night kids played and kicked balls. She rarely ventured here for that exact reason.

Kids. For a woman who'd been handed the café when young, control over fertility had been an assumed right. But that, like so many things, could be swiftly altered; stolen like a prized possession snatched without due sanction or preparation. Like her recent bombshell.

Premature Ovarian Failure. The words rattled around in her brain, clunky and surreal. Not true, surely? But the diagnosis was recent enough to feel more alien than processed.

'Mummy, mummy — catch me if you can!' yelled a small girl in a yellow rain-jacket, her hair the exact mousy mixture Callie had once fancifully imagined her dream daughter might have. The realisation sliced into her tender heart tissue. Such thoughts tore her and revealed naïve notions she'd been crazy to entertain.

'*A rare condition in a young woman. It affects only one in a thousand women below twenty-nine. The average age of onset is your age, twenty-seven. You may still have children — but the chances are severely diminished. I'm sorry this will have come as a shock.*' The doctor's words echoed razor-sharp as Callie turned, unwanted tears smarting. She'd only booked the routine check-up after a run of absent periods. The life-altering diagnosis still left her feeling bereft.

'Mummy, chase me!' yelled the toddler.

Callie's hands clutched the keys in her pocket so hard she hurt her skin. She abandoned the driftwood where she'd stood, not wanting to see the girl whirled in her mother's arms, giggling with delight. The child made her recognise just how much she craved a family of her own.

Callie walked, ignoring her streaming tears. She wondered if being motherless herself made her yearn for that special bond. Or was it that her grandparents had given her such unconditional acceptance that she ached to play such a crucial role? Or had her father's abandonment created the yearning? Somehow she'd always known that having a family of her own would be her greatest achievement.

Now her assumptions lay shattered with the diagnosis that her fertility had dwindled already. Defects in her hormones might likely mean such a child would never be hers.

She'd plaster on a fake smile for this evening; there was no other choice. She had to learn to live a full life without fruitless future dreams. With a heavy heart, she walked back to the café, not wanting to face a planned future plunged into black; not wanting anything that life offered her.

★   ★   ★

Heat and the scent of sweet pastries baking enveloped them both. For Hamish, watching Callie's face highlighted by the early morning sun kicked the temp past anything the oven could push out. He held back a flood of longing as he watched Callie ice pastry wafers in her kitchen: steady attention, exact precision. His palms twitched to tug her close for the embrace he dreamed of enveloping her in.

But that would never happen, unless she had her disappointment in him purged. And that made his stomach's knots multiply to hard-to-bear point. Courtroom challenges were way preferable to being emotionally ransacked and on the back foot with Callie.

A to-do sign flashed in his future. *Get over this. She doesn't want you.* The lingering unrequited longing came with a bitter regrets reminder. Callie wore her dislike like an all-body tattoo. He ignored his urge to tug her close and kiss away her angst; to make her laugh and drop that *crème pâtissière* piping bag as he turned her to steal a kiss. Callie continued icing, unaware of his personal fantasies and inner maelstrom.

Hamish unglued his tongue. 'Anything I can do for you?'

'Could you go along to Oliver's and get supplies?' she asked without taking her attention from her work.

Hamish rearranged his frazzled brain cells. 'Sure. Your quest is my pleasure.' He always aimed for chirpy, flirty chap. It charmed the women — except for Callie. Surface banter didn't cut her depths. He knew; he'd tried often with no reward.

She kept icing without ceasing her work flow. He yearned to pull her around and seize her full attention.

'We're running low on loo rolls. Oliver's has my shopping list. Take my car; keys on the hook with the campervan keyring. She can be reluctant to start, but give it a minute if she stalls. That okay?' Still Callie didn't look up.

'You still drive a VW campervan?'

'Yes. And your point is?'

'Still give it a crazy name too, I'll bet.' He moved closer, risking a waft of her strawberry scent. The one that speared his gut.

'Lots of people do. All the best people.'

He slid nearer. His hands twitched; the brush of his thumb on her arm would satisfy his craving. But he knew if he did she'd knock him out. 'But do you ever go anywhere in it? Bet you still don't. You never change, Cal. What's this one called, anyway?'

Her fingers stopped. He was gratified to have sparked a reaction. 'She's called Violet,' she said, her expression animated with *blow him away* twinkling enthusiasm. 'Inside she's purple. Even the curtains. There's lavender Highland mountains and lochs painted around the ceiling . . . even a stag. Got an art student on board. Scottish campervan supreme.'

Hamish's brain reeled off an impetuous mini-film. Him playing the hero, taking her away in that campervan and treating her like his Scots princess. He stifled a snort. Like the independent Ms. Dewar would allow *his* help.

'I'll take my motorbike. Kilted bikers always get the girls. Purple campervan can't compete.' He watched her hand curl tight around the icing bag as her knuckles whitened. How did he manage to make her so tense?

She stared as irritation flashed in her sapphire eyes. 'You'll make a mockery of my business, Hamish. I'd rather you didn't do that. You'd get attention for all the wrong reasons.'

'Kidding, Cal. Sense of humour bypass? You were fun once.' His voice sounded clipped and flippant. 'They say men are from Mars, but you act like you're set on buying me a one-way ticket back. I'm trying to be friendly here. White flag waving under your nose, too.'

She turned away, her frustration camouflaged. 'You've always been reckless. Too quick to joke.'

'Now play nice.' He'd even tried to forget her — erase her from his brain's hard drive; or that was what he'd told himself. But it hadn't stopped her creeping into his dreams, or the turbo-hitch in his pulse whenever he saw an elfin-haired blonde. Dammit. *And now I'm back and you despise me. Nice slice!*

Her eyes were back on the regimentally lined patisserie. He could read the subtext: *Get out and leave me alone.* 'Can you fetch those supplies now please?' she said.

Hamish clutched his heart. 'And I was going to ask you if you fancied fish and chips from Cromars's tonight, on me. Chips . . . sauce . . . my riveting company. I'll even include curry sauce if you're being super-demanding.'

Callie's hand stilled. Under that awful chef's cap, he knew her hair was blonde and baby-soft. Not letting him touch was a criminal act.

'I'm backed up. Thanks but no.'

'I can put in an advance order. Large portion, from the wrapper. By the shore with the seagulls bombing. Like old times.'

She stared at him, piping bag in hand. 'You need to get back to your proper job, Hamish.' Then she put the bag down. 'Why are you back in Fife, anyway? You've never explained the sudden urge to revisit your past.'

'Fancied a change. Hankered for home. Nice to see you missed me and enjoy my company so much you have to ask. As it happens, I'm thinking of a return to Scotland.' He smiled, but the confession didn't get any reaction.

31

'Back to small-time law work? Won't you be bored? You can do so much better.'

He shrugged. 'Thinking I could try something new. Maybe even set up work here in St. Andrews. Settle back home.'

Her fingers seized the bag again but trembled. 'You should focus on your career. This is a comedown. And the café's way beneath your abilities. As much as I'm grateful you stepped in, I can manage. So you can move on now if you need to.'

'I'm happy staying — it's fun, believe it or not.'

Her face darkened. 'I'm uncomfortable with your work style. I can't reprimand you when you're working for free. So I'm suggesting we part ways soon. I'm grateful to you for stepping in, but I can tell you have issues about your future to deal with.'

'Ah, I get it. That was direction over a suggestion. When do you want me to finish?' He felt winded, as if her slight had stabbed him in the midriff. And inside he bled out while she counted the minutes until he went.

She watched him, solemn as a church bell tolling remembrance. 'End of the week?' She narrowed her eyes. 'Use the time to organise your future. Or take a break. Thanks for the help you've given me.'

'If that's what you want, yes I'll leave.' Hamish watched the woman who'd been on his mind too often. 'For your info, I have no plans, except maybe getting you to say yes to a last supper. I'll fill you in on my riveting nonexistent future, and in return you can tell me why you're so fed up that I barely see you smile lately, let alone laugh. Fish, chips and therapy with an old friend. A perfect combo. A last goodbye.'

She stopped. 'I do smile.'

'Not much. And frankly that's pretty sad. Come on . . . join me just to celebrate the fact I've just agreed to leave, if you must.'

She inhaled deeply and restarted her work. 'I honestly can't. Please fetch the supplies. That's all I need from you now.'

Yep, he had the moves; women swooned. And while he'd aced everything in life, his major exception was in getting the girl. Hamish needed his head flushed of his hopeless cravings for Callie Dewar. He was as hung-up as ever on her, yet his love life was down the drain. Loo rolls said it all.

'Be back before you know I'm gone.'

'Please don't rush on my account,' she answered.

★ ★ ★

The next morning proved busy, since two touring groups had nominated The Caledonian Cupcake Café as their brunch stop. The hard rush meant Callie could avoid a certain chatty kilted waiter again causing static at her serving hatch.

'Boss, going to turn that frown upside down today?' he chided.

'I'm fine. I'd be better if you worked faster.'

'You're scaring the customers.' His grin rattled her, but she donned a neutral expression that faked untold patience.

'Did I tell you you're the boss I love to tease?'

'You're too busy annoying me to say anything useful.'

Callie forced herself to concentrate. Already there was a sizeable line and double parking in the cobbled street outside. Maybe there was a golf event at the famous Old Course, only a short walk away. As a habit, they warned of traffic-warden penalties on their chalkboard, but today either nobody cared or tea was their primary goal.

She fixed Hamish with a warning stare. 'Speed up. We're too busy to chat. I'll smile when the line's handled.'

Today Hamish sported stubble, tousled hair and an over-friendly mood. Trying not to stare at the feast he presented in his gunmetal shirt and Black Watch kilt combo, Callie found herself being eyed by the striking peacocks in Grandad's art-deco stained décor glass. Ironic that Hamish strutted as proudly. And suddenly the décor she'd salvaged and had so much affection for since childhood mocked her from the coffee bar and ramped up her irritation.

'Shame not to embrace the joy of this fine day,' he remarked.

Callie gritted her teeth. 'Table seven are hungry. Get to it. Are you only interested in service when it's an all-female table?'

'The ladies have the best tips and biggest smiles.' Hamish grinned, flashing super-white teeth. 'I'm even being nice to the boss who wants me gone.'

Callie comforted herself with the knowledge that this emotional assault had a time limit. Her other waiters, Callum Baxter and Gregor Jamieson, could be relied upon to fill in until a replacement arrived. Both were using this as a stepping stone into hospitality training. Unlike Hamish, they didn't cross lines.

After queuing to be seated, six bubbling all-American golfer girls entered, their designer sports ensembles a confection of peaches, pinks and baby blues. Fortunately a couple of tables had come free, and the boys arranged chairs to accommodate them together. Their animated chatter was as infectiously bright as their costumes.

'Hey — the plaid in this place is neat.' They gushed over Callie's salvaged mismatched tartan chairs, sofas and shabby-chic café fixtures.

'My mom would adore it.'

'I want a slice of all the cakes. Those puffy macaroons look awesome.'

Hearing their chatter, and despite her busy shift, Callie reflected on her small but busy empire. It boasted only twenty tables, with stripped wooden floors, globe lights, dado rails, and assorted mixed tartan and upcycled pine tables for a retro edge. But it made her heart swell to hear its humble charms praised. Yes, she might get grumpy about her business squeezing her at times, but she had proud moments too.

'I need to buy a stag sculpture like that to take home. Super-cute! Are you open to offers, or do I have to steal him in my bag? You're pretty cute too, Cute Waiter In a Kilt.' The enquirer first pointed at the stag ornament on the mantel, but then directed her question at Hamish with a wide grin. He had the decency to look bashful.

'That's flattering, but I don't think I'd fit. In your bag, that is.'

Callie's heart zoomed from pride to pique. Hamish always managed to grab the full spotlight.

The girl played right along. 'Ooh. I'd be pushing luggage allowance limits, but it'd be worth it. Anyone else wanna share?' Which only made the group giggle and whoop.

'Ladies, welcome to Callie's Café.' Hamish dazzled the party with his signature smile. 'I'm Hamish. I'll be your server this morning. I hope you enjoy your visit.' He distributed menus as the women watched with doe eyes.

'Linger over the menu choices and I'll return to guide you further.'

Callie ignored the ensuing drooling and focused on prepping her tiered cake and sandwich plates. Her triangular sandwiches nestled beside strawberry tarts and edible flower cupcakes. But while her work was neat, inside she was a tangled ball of wrath. Did he toy with her nerves on purpose? Or was he so completely oblivious to the dampened fire that blazed every time he was near? The depth of feelings she still had for this man were both a marvel and a burden that caused churning emotions. And as Hamish wasn't cooling the flirt factor anytime soon, would she last to the end of the week?

'So, ladies — may I make recommendations from our specials? Our soup of the day is lentil-and-roasted-pepper with home-baked breads. Or I urge you to try the cranachan tier cake, or macaroons trio with salted caramel sauce.'

Callie rolled her eyes at Jonty. 'He

has more gush than a water-treatment-centre flood.'

'He's their hot Scot dream come true,' said Jonty. 'Face it, he brings in crowds. Cakes and kilts are a winning combination.'

'Hamish. Service. Now.'

Kilt swinging, he carried the tea-things high with the finesse of a Michelin-star waiter, displaying legs fit for a Highland games field and a male-model profile. Women nudged each other as he passed.

Callie chided herself for watching when she had so much work to do. A large TV van drew up in the street and her customers craned to watch. She then recognised the blonde who exited the vehicle as Hamish's admirer from the day before who'd taken so long at her table that Callie had had to nudge him about it. She watched the woman walk inside and up to Hamish for a verbal exchange. *Not again!*

Half a minute later, Hamish approached the servery and took in a deep breath. 'I need to ask a favour . . . Lana works for Scottish TV. They're in St. Andrews covering a golf story, but it's a slow news day. They want kilts and cupcakes as the latest Scottish 'to do', for tonight's news. That okay, boss? Apparently it's international cupcake day.'

Callie stared hard. 'We're snowed under with work. I'm not sure.'

'It's a great chance for your business. It's amazing prime-time attention.'

But something burned in Callie's head that couldn't allow her to be grateful or compliant. Maybe it was the fact that she was busy, tired and preoccupied. Or that Hamish held this blonde media-whiz goddess in such thrall that he'd move mountains to help her.

'Prior warning might have helped, you know. Being a pal of yours doesn't mean your friend can take the helm.'

Hamish's eyes accused her with a dark glare. 'This is an opportunity, not a problem. Why do you turn everything round?'

Jonty came up, buzzing with the news. 'Cal, think of the publicity. Scottish TV! You'll be famous. People will flock if they see this on the news. I'll help — all hands on deck. It'll really put you on the map.'

Callie shook her head. 'The customers waiting outside will leave. That's business lost if I ignore it.'

Hamish shrugged. 'How about I deliver a free drink? We have spare fudge samples from the rep; they could have those as a complimentary treat. The customers won't mind if they know there are people from the TV here, especially if we make a fuss over them. It's a bit of fame and fun we can all enjoy.'

Callie felt unable to disagree amid such enthusiasm. But she felt undervalued and tawdry next to Ms. Media Superstar, Lana. Even her name reeked Hollywood.

What was it with Hamish that he always seized power? Why did she react so badly, and always jump to conclusions about his affections lying elsewhere? In a blink, the feelings of being railroaded and overwhelmed transported her right back to the night he'd told her they could never have a future. Also the fact that the TV blonde was now hanging on Hamish's arm and whispering in his ear.

Callie saw red and was about to fire them down when the blonde butted in before Callie could give Hamish any more direction. 'My editor wants a piece on cupcakes and kilts. I particularly want the men featured — interviews and shots of diners. Maybe a vox pop of people outside. We may have you explain how this started if you freshen your spattered chef's clothes. Messy isn't a good image. Do you have a change we could use?'

Callie's insides tumbled. This was her café. She sanctioned all events. She might be messy, but she worked hard, and this was *her business baby.*

The blonde raised beauty-room-perfected eyebrows. 'Image is all,' Lana the TV guru decreed, holding her microphone like a sceptre indicating her media-diva status.

Callie inhaled to summon calm. 'Yes, you can interview my staff. But you should've asked me first. I don't want to be interviewed at length. And the customers must give their consent to being filmed, too. Do those rules sound workable for you?'

Hamish touched her arm and the spot zinged with heat. 'It'll be great, trust me. You've got to be interviewed — it's your chance, Callie. Seize it.'

'I'll rustle up some treats for the queue outside,' Jonty butted in. 'The business association will be overjoyed, Cal. Your gramps would've been proud of you.'

With injustice burning an acid pit inside her, Callie relented. But her heart felt tight with sadness as she watched Hamish run after Lana like a puppy dog. Why was she so invisible to the man who kept her up nights? And why did she feel in danger of letting her lip tremble at the way it made her feel such loss?

Wasn't she better off letting him go when she had such a blighted future?

One conviction rose inside her. She was way better than petty jealousy over Hamish, and she'd squash it now and take charge. Her café, her rules. Callie walked out into the centre of the room and addressed her clients.

'We're being filmed for tonight's TV news. I know I can count on my loyal customers to rise to this opportunity. Today's orders are on the house. Please stay and help show off the best café in St. Andrews with me.'

'Hear, hear!' Maisie Weir endorsed nearby, while another table started a rousing round of applause. Feeling inner butterflies swoop, Callie returned to her kitchen, knowing Hamish's grey gaze never left her.

She raised a brow to stamp authority. 'So let's prove we're an unstoppable team!'

3

Callie went to the local pharmacy for headache pills. The pulsing that had started earlier during filming was now a pounding thunderstorm that threatening to overwhelm her if she didn't act. Hamish could take the blame there too.

She reached the chemist, but something on the periphery of her vision stopped her in her tracks. Linley crouched as she perused the products on the low shelf and read the packets carefully. Callie knew with certainty what she held in her hand, and she figured her best friend would want to use the pregnancy test before divulging anything.

Callie realised she still held her breath. A sharp flash slammed across her temples and winded her with the pain of a migraine. Her hand grabbed the door frame, while a knot tightened painfully in her stomach at what she'd just happened upon. Could she push through and meet her best friend in this way? She wanted to be happy for Linley, but confusion swept her away in a tsunami tide of angst.

Callie retreated. Sure she hadn't been seen, she turned and hurried away. She'd go the long way back to her café and pop into another shop that stocked paracetamol. She so wanted to be overjoyed about her best friend's situation, but she'd no real reason to explain the tears that ran down her face.

Babies. Baby news was part of life. She'd never have the opportunity to share such an event. She'd never experience such joy. Instead she'd have to get used to this 'iron skin acceptance' and develop a fake smile to cope. And she'd somehow work on finding a mask of joy to see her through the tough times.

Just not quite yet. She was still too tender to find her way forward. And that pain was way worse than any migraine.

★ ★ ★

Her headache eased, Callie tapped Hamish's shoulder. The slight contact burned, but she kept her resolve firm even when his grey questioning gaze met hers. She directed him to the kitchen door with a nod. 'Hamish — we need to talk.'

The camera team had filmed in her café for over an hour. They'd homed in on the American golfer girls, who rose admirably to the challenge of being filmed and interviewed, praising the establishment to the rafters. At one stage a mini-ceilidh with the kilted servers had turned the café into a party venue when Jonty had turned up the stereo. Callie had asked Jonty to set her TV record box to capture the evening news.

But now that the moment of fame had passed, Callie felt drained. Inner doubts nagged, but she was firm as she beckoned Hamish to her kitchen. The moment had come. When they arrived, she straightened her spine, glad her chef's hat hid her train-wreck hair. The ordeal of talking on camera and getting her words in a mix made all else pale.

Hamish's startling grey gaze searched hers, and she knew he'd read her purpose when he laid down his pad and pen and then untied the apron he donned for cleaning duty.

'I need straight answers,' she began. 'Did you let Lana arrange this without my consent? Call it a hunch, but indulge me please. Did you know about this when she came in before, but you didn't tell me? Is that why her first visit here took so long?'

Hamish pressed his lips together, then sighed but didn't reply. He nodded. 'It was for the simple reason that I'm trying my best to help you.'

Why do you let others pull your strings, yet you never listen to me? Why am I invisible? Aloud she said, 'I knew it.' A taper ignited inside her at his high-handed meddling. Hamish's jaw flexed, then he looked away. 'What made you do that? I'm in charge. Me. Why don't you get that? What's wrong with you that you fail to see it?'

He shook his head. 'She told me she wanted to come back. I would've told you, but you were in a nightmare mood with knobs on, and you disappeared before my shift ended. I feel like you're angry with me, and I figured you'd have used some excuse or taken offence. And you'd only have lost your greatest-ever chance at publicity.'

'So Hamish knows best?' *Nightmare mood. Taken offence. Another lost chance.* His words rang around her head like a taunting chant, goading her that she'd always lose with Hamish when other women only crooked a finger and he ran to obey. Losing was her life motto right now. She'd lost her biggest-ever dream. The one where she'd find a man who loved her enough to have kids with her.

Hamish inhaled to continue, but she held up a hand. 'You give me no credit for being a force in this place. I could have prepped and managed things. You give me no credit for managing a business I own.'

'Would you, though Cal? My bet is you'd've said no point-blank. You always do, especially when it's me who's asking.'

Callie jabbed at her now-heaving bosom. 'This is my café — nobody else but me has kept it open and still alive after years of Gramps's business slowly going downhill. I alone have the right to decide. I make the decisions. This place may not be much, but it's still mine.'

Injustice burned like a pyre near her heart. She'd worked her behind off here. Lost out on a proper catering education. Missed holidays. Seen relationships fail. All because the café came first. And now she was being treated like she didn't count when she'd put her damn future on hold for a café that had always felt destined to teeter towards failure.

His stare slashed hers. 'Oh we know.

Your café. And you bear it like a cross.'

Did he really just say that? Callie's eyes widened. 'What did you say? I may not have fancy qualifications to rival yours, but I know more about this place than you ever will.' They stood toe to toe. He was tall, but she wasn't backing down an inch.

'You've been so busy telling me you want me out, and that you don't like my methods, when the bottom line is that you need this business to be a success — and this profile boost is the best chance you've got. I suggested that Lana consider the café as a novelty filler. She fell for it, and I wasn't going to wreck your chance. In another dimension you'd see I'm right. But right now you'll never admit it, because you have it in your head that I'm a nuisance, and that nobody's up to this job but you.'

Callie watched that firm chest rise and fall with the passion behind his words. 'See? Even now, no apology,' she accused, her voice rising like a bird that bore her anger up and up and up. 'You're a piece of work.'

'I'm sorry I came here to do you favours. I'm done.'

She was too far gone with the injustice of how he'd painted her to feel he deserved to be the injured party. He didn't pay her the respect she was owed. He always took the upper hand. And he never saw it, no matter how many times they argued. She pulled herself to full height and put a hand on his chest — a warm, firm chest, worked out in all the right ways. And the fact that her body responded, betraying her, made her regretful. So she raised her voice. 'I want you to go. We don't work well together. You're out of here. Go now.'

Hamish shook his head as he turned away. 'This isn't about the café, or the filming, or me being your worst waiter; it's about us. You have some auto-eject anti-Hamish thing going on, and you have done for years.'

'Get over yourself.'

He held up a stalling hand. 'Let me finish. You need to get over it. You don't have to ask me again; I've had more than I can take. Have a nice in-control but OCD life, Callie.' He put up his hands, this time in surrender. Then he backed out and the door swung shut after him.

She'd got her wish as she turned with shaking hands and let the angry tears fall. Was she screwing up everything right now? Was the avalanche of her diagnosis and life woes blinding her?

Whatever. Hamish's rebel reign was over. But his words still stung. He blamed her for everything. Maybe he was right . . . He'd recognised her troubles and figured she was the root cause of them. And the worst part was she knew he had a point. She hated her predicament. She was ejecting him from the café when she should be leaving it herself. Because her future had crashed with a doctor's shock words — and she kept the secret hurt hidden while her life fell apart.

* * *

In her quiet after-hours café, Callie presented the plate before her guest, knowing this encounter was the start of the negative consequences of her actions. Flora Gordon was an eighty-one-year-old with attitude who had flamboyant taste in tartan capes and hats. Her energy was as vibrant as her fashion taste, and today she sported an ensemble of blues and claret red.

Several staff had gone home voicing their disappointment at Hamish's sudden departure. Now Callie had to deal with another telling-off, this time from his aunt.

'Enjoy these, Flora. I kept your favourite cakes for you, which was tricky during a mad rush. We've never been busier.'

Hamish's Aunt Flora was a regular customer who didn't mince words or dally with diplomacy. 'Saw you all on the news — quite a to-do you've had today. And Linley told me about the after-filming fall-out. So, you sacked him. Why have you let yourself get into such a snit? Sounds like the day from hissy-fit hell.'

'Can we not talk about it?' Callie polished tables that didn't need cleaning. But Flora's interrogation left her needing to escape. She wasn't about to confess her inner feelings about Flora's favourite nephew anytime soon. The cloth in her hand felt therapeutic, and it helped keep her gaze averted.

'This isn't like you, Callie. What got into you?'

'Let's say Hamish doesn't understand the idea of having a boss. And don't get me started on the flirting . . .'

'Sit down,' the older woman commanded. 'You don't need to tell me; Linley's filled me in. That lad needs a lesson in stepping away from centre stage and taking orders. Of course, having gushing women panting after him all day will have gone to his head and made him overstep. But that's not the point. He got out of line, but he wouldn't have meant any disrespect.

You've clearly let a bad situation spin out of control.'

Callie sat and looked at her. She had no words she wanted to say. 'It's too late to go back, for either of us. I don't even want to talk about it.'

'The question is,' said Flora, 'when are you going to act like a grown-up and speak up about this crush you've had on each other for forever?'

Surprising her into a jolt, Callie stared at Flora and sat up poker-straight. Had Flora really just said that out loud? And who had told her things Callie hadn't even admitted to herself? 'Now you're being ridiculous,' she said.

Flora's cheeks puffed. 'Am I? You were in love with my nephew when you were a schoolgirl. You think you can conceal it, but I can see beneath the act. He always had a soft spot for his wee Callie Dewar, and I thought the two of you would end up married. Denied hidden ardour causes problems, which you seem to be discovering after all these years.'

57

'Flora, can we not go there?'

The older woman harrumphed. 'Why pretend? I suggest now is as good a time as any to get to the bones of this beef. I'm going to call him — '

Callie put out a hand to stop her. 'Don't. The dust needs to settle. Please, respect my wishes.'

'I'm old, not blind. He's as bad as you are. He's back here trying to get your attention, and you're still angry at him for leaving you in the first place. He's called off his engagement. Pretty thing, but sad eyes for a girl with a new ring on her finger. I don't think his heart was in it at all. He's too in love with you.'

Callie's voice was a low whisper as her mind did cartwheels about what Flora had just revealed. 'Now you're having mad notions.'

'Enough of your cheek, lassie.'

She'd never taken issue with Flora before — she wouldn't dare to out of respect for her seniors, and Flora was the matriarch of the Gordon family. But this micro-examination of her most private feelings wasn't permitted. How did Flora see so much? Callie's first instinct was to blame herself — she'd been too readable, obviously. And that made her mind race as weariness sapped her muscles and her heart was wounded by the events of the day.

Flora's gaze still searched her own. 'I sacked Hamish,' Callie said, 'and I'm not going to talk about it any more, even if I was interested. We'd be the worst people in the world to get together.'

Flora took off her tartan cape and poured another cup of Earl Grey. Was she planning on being here for the night to beat Callie into submission? Flora was way off beam if she thought she'd win. Callie resisted her pressing urge to scream.

The older woman sipped again from the rosebud cup, then picked up a mini-eclair and devoured it. 'You both remind me of me and my Keith. We were chalk and cheese, but we loved each other with a fierce depth. Go and speak to Hamish; tell him you like him, give yourself permission to try. You're in your late twenties and both acting like toddlers. Stop it. There — I've said enough.'

The heat in Callie's cheeks at Flora's startling reprimand told her she might deny all she liked, but it wasn't going to convince the woman. Callie trusted her views and opinions, but on this her elderly friend didn't have the full facts. There were no rose-tinted endings to be had, not in her new-version future. How could a chap who'd done so well with everything he'd tried take the tragedy of her diagnosis as a relation-ship starting point? There was no way she was disclosing it to any of them, so Flora's romantic dreams were com-pletely unfounded. The reminder of it all hurt a great deal.

Flora's gaze glittered back. 'I'm right, and I always get my way. Stop evading. Wake up. You're meant to be together, and for some crazy reason you keep fighting against it. For what it's worth, he might fancy himself a lot — but he loves you much more. What will we do with the pair or you?'

'You're wrong,' Callie insisted. 'If you saw the way he acts with women in front of me, you'd know it. Anyway, I don't care as long as he stays away from me. We are not destined to ever be a match.'

Flora nibbled a macaroon before proceeding. 'He's trying to get your attention, lassie. And you're in denial. I don't intend to give up on this — but first I have a proposition for you.'

'Do I have a choice?' Callie said, now feeling desperate.

Flora searched in her bag and removed an ornate thistle keyring, which she handed over with an aged brown envelope. 'I want to offer you my cottage as a holiday location. Linley's put things in place for you to go. I'm giving you no reason not to accept. Think of this as a thank-you for years of entertaining a lonely old lady with company and tea and cakes. It's yours — a cottage near Glencoe and Fort William; the only neighbours are sheep and Ben Nevis. Don't worry; there's running water and electricity. You might just love it, and if nothing else it'll be a sanctuary for rest.'

Callie stared at her hard. 'You know how much I adore you, but I don't think I can accept your offer. If it's meant to persuade me about Hamish, it won't work.'

'It has nothing to do with the lad. You can't go on working yourself into an early breakdown. Go to Glencoe; get your head in order. Have a rest. You can't go on as you are, lass, so take the key.'

Callie's emotions swelled raw and pure at this unexpected gift. It was an offer more welcome than Flora knew. She watched her elderly friend with eyes she knew glistened with tears she'd tried to hold back. Could she do this? She had café cover in place thanks to Linley. Now she had no reason to say no.

'No strings? No Hamish persuasion? I can't go if that's your plan, as much as I do want the trip.'

'All you have to do is turn up and light a fire. My friend Agnes has stocked it up. It's there when you want it, with a claw foot bath and open fires. Why would you turn away from that? With one of the best views in all the Scottish Highlands on your doorstep?'

Callie felt gratitude burn bright, and the flicker of opportunity she yearned to grasp as her heart squeezed with joy. 'I'll pay.'

'If you do, I'll never speak to you again. Go spoil yourself with my blessing. Linley told me she's bringing a chef in plus his assistant; you'll meet them tomorrow. A day showing him the ropes and you're free as a bird. Your café will be in good hands — and so will you!'

Callie blew out a breath. 'You ganging up to wear me down?' She longed to be alone with stunning views, a pile of books, and a cosy bed with no work. For quiet and calm. To think and to plan. And all her arguments were being ably answered.

Flora stood slowly, picked up her cape and smiled as Callie helped her back into it. 'I prefer to think of it as friends looking out for the ones they love, lassie. And you are loved, if you'll allow it.'

Callie caught sight of her drawn, weary reflection in the mirror above the hearth. 'I sometimes feel like life's crushing me, one cream-scone plate at a time. I could do with an amicable separation from this place. You may be right.'

'The Dewar business has stood here for decades. It won't decline into ash and dust if you have the audacity to take a break, now, will it?'

Callie smiled then hugged her. 'You Gordons don't give in. Okay, Glencoe it is — and thank you. Thank you so very much.'

Flora flicked off cake crumbs before she grasped her walking cane. 'Then that's arranged. And now I must go; I've other business to attend to.'

Callie could only wonder at what other marvels Flora had planned. Whoever it was wouldn't stand a chance of saying no.

4

Getting love-life advice from an octogenarian really wasn't a life high-point, Callie decided. She drove past gorgeous Highland postcard views that inspired wonder and reflection while her mind revisited Flora's recent words; most specifically the accusation of a lingering crush on Hamish, which bothered her more than she liked.

As a girl she'd wanted him, but he'd made his disinterest in her cuttingly plain. They'd got together when she was seventeen, with disastrous results. A surprise party kiss culminated in him doing a U-turn and telling her he'd made a mistake. Mortification burned her memory even now. *'This shouldn't have happened, Cal. Pretend it didn't. I can't do this.'*

Romantic notions about Hamish were way off beam. Her resulting back-off and emotional barricade had worked — until now. Until he'd returned with a covert plan to vex her. So Linley and Flora had it all wrong. And his accusations about her job scraped at her conscience too. He saw the hurt in her too ably; sensed her tender spot. But there was no way she was ready to confide her secrets.

As if dealing a final reprimand, a bang sounded beneath Callie somewhere under the van and made her jump, heart pounding. She gripped the wheel with white knuckles. 'What else can go wrong on me now?'

Violet, Callie's trusty but clunky purple vintage vehicle, chose that moment to issue a low clanking bang that made Callie wince and caused it to reach a complete standstill.

'Please don't die, Vi. Push through; I need this escape.'

Violet's ignition clicked limply and refused to re-engage.

'Please start. You know you want to. For me. Pretty please.'

Callie grabbed her road atlas. Flora's cottage lay beyond Glencoe and Fort William in the village of Spean Bridge, past the mountain sprawl of Ben Nevis. But she hadn't even got to Fort William yet, and Violet had voted to stay in Ballachulish and never budge again.

'Oh Violet, so much for teamwork.' At least she was on the small village's outskirts and might be able to summon help. She tried the ignition once more without response, thankful for a space to freewheel the vehicle into.

Callie had encountered too many 'silent stuck moments' lately. Work; her diagnosis. But for once she wasn't worrying about her café. That was in great hands thanks to Claude Debeau and his able assistant, Chloe. Giving them instructions hadn't taken long. At one time she'd have struggled to let go, but now she was so keen to escape she'd probably have handed the keys to a cake-making clown circus and a team of kilted monkeys. She'd agreed to a four-day break with a possibility of extending it and moving on with the van — only that now seemed unlikely.

She got out of the vehicle, as there was no way she could push it further. Stretching her limbs, she took in the majesty of her surroundings. She should treat this as a detour instead of a pitfall. The journey through Glencoe had been a movie-set-perfect drive anchoring her thoughts, while a betraying mental voice asked, *Has Hamish been here before?*

Now her breakdown brought a fresh challenge. 'Maybe if I wait, Violet might recover.' Callie decided to head to the nearest pub and work out a van-fix plan later. She retrieved her jacket, rucksack and essentials, then tried the ignition again without response.

★ ★ ★

The pub was rustic, and the kind of place where fashion makeovers every few years to compete with trends were a foreign tongue. Some might have described it as dingy, but a conservatory area at the back lent some light to an otherwise dark wood-panelled bar. Only a couple of tables were occupied.

All heads swivelled to look when the door closed loudly behind Callie. Oops. Maybe strangers weren't welcome, she thought. Well, too bad. She had no campervan for a fast escape; she'd have to brazen it out. She straightened her spine and walked with conviction to the bar.

'Good afternoon. Are you still serving lunch?' she enquired in her best friendly voice as she inched towards a bar stool.

The barman raised a dark brow at her. A quirk of his lip hinted at a sense of humour beneath the gruff façade. He was youngish, his hair collar-length and wavy, but he had bright blue startling eyes, and his mouth began to morph into an almost appealing hint of smile as he watched her.

'New? Tourist, are you? We don't get many tourists coming in here,' he said as if she'd fallen off the edge of a map. 'We don't do fancy cocktails, if that's what you're after.'

'No; I'm having a bit of car trouble. My mobile is low on charge, too.'

'Shame. We have a payphone out back.'

'You have a lunch menu, I take it?'

'Limited, but the locals like it. We try not to poison people.' He slid the menu her way as if offering her some prized tome from a vault. He placed the cloth he'd been polishing glasses with down on the bar. 'I'm afraid the cook's just clocked off. His wife's pet goat's gone AWOL. And it eats everything it can find, so it's an emergency hereabouts.'

Callie shuddered. 'I have an aversion to goats. And sheep, actually. Don't ask me to help with a search party.'

'Scared of sheep? I've never heard anything dafter.' With widened eyes, he looked at her like she'd just announced she'd signed a contract for a space-cult timeshare on the moon.

'A brush with an angry one when I

71

was small,' Callie explained. 'It left mental scars.' She winced, not wanting to revisit the terror and the bruises when she'd fallen face down in a field.

'You won't be tempted by lamb-and-mint-flavoured crisps then,' the barman teased. She wrinkled her nose. 'I can just about grate cheese for a sandwich or ploughman's, if you care to risk your life,' he added.

She placed her chin on her hand as she pondered her choices. 'Are your sandwiches so bad they need a health warning? The board outside said 'tasty home-made food'. You may need to revise it to 'meals best eaten with care'.'

'You're funny for a lass who's stranded and at my mercy.' His smile fully appeared, and Callie knew he was definitely laughing at her.

She grinned back. 'I know. I've nothing to lose. So I'll opt for the sandwich, since you made it sound so tantalising. And that bottled ginger beer looks sensational after half an hour shouting at a van engine. Can I have it in a glass with ice, please?'

He was still smiling, but his eyebrow-lift told her he now thought she might be quite mad. 'Cheese and chutney, or ham? I think I have a bag of salad in the fridge if you're nice. Take a seat. I'm Fraser, by the way.'

She opted for a cheese-salad sandwich as safest. 'I'm Callie, and I'm headed for Spean Bridge. I'm frustratingly near, too, but my campervan has other ideas about me making it there.'

'What year VW?' he asked her in a reverent voice that suggested she'd just happened on a fellow obsessive. He stared at her with the most attention he'd given her since her arrival.

They talked VW for the next ten minutes flat, and Fraser expressed an interest in seeing Violet for himself. Callie figured he probably frequented chat-rooms about them, and that was a sad enough plight in itself. He also told her he was an enthusiast, and said he refurbished vehicles and held enthusiast 'meets'.

'You're lucky you came by.' he said. 'I can take a look. And if I can't fix it, then I know somebody who can. You should see the collection in my yard.'

So destiny, or Violet, had brought them to the right place after all, she thought. Had Violet sensed a VW guardian angel? 'I'd appreciate your wisdom. And of course I'll pay for your time and any parts you need. Make the ginger beer a double. Let's push the boat out; I'm feeling like we can do this!'

Fraser grinned at her. 'Any VW fangirl is welcome in my bar. Refreshments coming right up for Callie the stranded Campervan Queen.'

⋆　⋆　⋆

Fraser couldn't fix Violet. He told her the technical terms for what needed doing, but she'd already tuned out and zoned onto topics more interesting, like bell-ringing and animal husbandry for crofters.

She blamed her lack of focus on the

awe-inspiring scenery as he drove her north in his own car. The Volkswagen Passat was way more modern than her vehicle, and hugely more comfortable and reliable. It would have been fun were it not for the too-loud metal music on the tinny stereo. Maybe she should reconsider her future vehicle choices, Callie thought. And maybe he should revisit his music tastes.

'So what you up here for?' Fraser asked.

'Holiday. A break. I've been working hard — I run a café, and my friend donated a cottage for a week. I just want to read and chill and sleep.'

'Sounds like you have great friends.'

'I do. Either that, or I was in such a bad mood they wanted rid of me.'

Fraser laughed. 'I doubt that. Fancy going out for a drink one night? I'll even wear smart clothes if you say yes.'

He slid her a look and Callie did a double-take. If she wasn't mistaken, he might just be flirting, or fishing. Her gaze slid down to check for a ring and none was present. But Fraser, though a nice chap with a kind and ready-to-help heart, just wasn't her type. He smelled of chip fat and engine oil. So what *was* her type exactly? Callie wondered.

'Maybe you'd fancy going out with me while you're here? Dinner even, or a movie? Or I could show you some local highlights. We could lie by the loch at night and listen to the wildcats.'

She'd rather join a convent. She pedalled for an escape route via small talk. 'Don't you work every night? I'd've thought bar work eats up a lot of free time.'

'I get two nights off. So what do you say? Will you risk it for a biscuit?'

'I'll think about it. I'll maybe just pop by the bar in the week for lunch when the cook is in, so I can attest to the menu quality. I can get a taxi. I might challenge you to make me a cocktail. Imagine the scandal.'

He gave her a look of mock offence. 'To think I almost opened a fresh jar of pickle for you.' He faked irritation.

'I sense you don't get many stray females walking into your bar usually. Do you always feel it necessary to ask them out, or am I a rare VW exception?'

'I think you're special.' He winked at her and she felt her face heat. 'I like talking nonsense with you, Callie. Even if you really don't deserve that van, given how little you know about how she works. It's pretty bad protocol not to be fully versed in your manual, you know?'

'Deal with it. And regarding the visit to the pub, we'll just have to wait and see.' Callie secretly wished she hadn't been so quick to promise.

They drove north from Fort William. The road took them out to the approach to Ben Nevis. 'Wow,' Callie breathed. 'My friend wasn't joking when she told me I'd be close to the mountain.'

'You a climber?'

'Never tried. I wouldn't dare on my own anyhow.'

'I could take you climbing.'

He was tenacious about taking her

out; she'd give him points for trying. 'Not sure. But thanks for the offer.'

They soon got to a new village, and Callie spied the sign for Spean Bridge, her destination at last. She felt her heart flutter in excitement that she was finally here and her holiday could begin.

'You can drop me here, where the shop is,' she said, determined to take in her locality without interruption. She had a map and her meagre bag of supplies.

'I'll take you to the cottage. It's no trouble.'

'I'd like to walk, and pick up some things in the local shop.'

'If you're sure.' He said it in a tone that made her think she'd maybe offended him.

'I really appreciate your kindness, and for being so patient and attentive. You earned your Good Samaritan badge helping me. Maybe I'll treat you to lunch — how does a double cheeseburger grab you?' She opened the door of the car and forced a smile.

'No payment needed, other than seeing you again. Bye, Callie. Take care of yourself. And see you soon, I hope.'

'Bye, Fraser.'

Watching him reverse the car and circle in the turning, Callie gritted her teeth as she set off for Bracken Cottage — key, map and optimism firmly in hand. She'd got through her vehicle malfunction. Now she'd have Flora's haven to herself for a week of splendid isolation.

* * *

Steam fogged the bathroom as Hamish set the shower jets to hot ultra-blast and flexed tired muscles from his run and firewood-chopping stint. He'd been gifted his aunt's cottage for the week; he needed the sanctuary.

From courteous café server to freakout kilted King Kong, he'd made a mess of things. So the solitude of Spean Bridge might regulate his temper and peace of mind.

Callie had fried his ability to watch her ruin her life. The woman made his radar bleep a toxic tantrum. For five days, Bracken Cottage offered respite. Maybe he'd take up the offer he'd had and go back to Strasbourg after all.

Sliding under the jets, Hamish groaned as hot pulsing water soothed a fraught mind and he soaped his skin — until a horror-film scream through the open window made him punch the shower's stop button with a closed fist. Was somebody being butchered outside Flora's house? The screaming was fit for a massacre.

Hamish jumped out dripping, snatched a towel, donning it as he ran, and took the stairs three at a time. Stopping only to grab a robe from the door hook, he sprinted through the backdoor, squinting in the sunlight to get his bearings.

More high-pitched screaming drew him to the front of the house. As Hamish rounded the corner, he slowed to stare as a snorting ram raced at an old oak tree and battered it with pounding hooves, its wrath at high level. It swiftly whirled round then butted again.

'Dornoch!' The ram was no stranger, but Hamish had never seen him in this mood — which he figured was largely fuelled by the screaming from high in the tree amid the leaves and branches. Again a high-pitched scream split his eardrums, and Hamish ran as close as was sensible with Dornoch raging. He felt too vulnerable in nothing but his aunt's towelling robe. The daffodil-yellow colour was so not his shade.

'Easy, Dornoch.' The local nomad ram was running fast in circles and repeat tree-butting. 'Guess I'm not the only one to erupt in crazy freak-out,' Hamish muttered. Frankly he could relate.

'Catch him — do it fast!' a female voice demanded, then screamed like she was aiming to smash windowpanes. He needed ear defenders to withstand the assault. She needed chill meds.

Hamish squinted at nightmare-scenario karma. 'Callie. Fancy meeting you here.'

'Catch him! Don't stand there — do

something!' Callie hung above him, her blonde-white hair swinging in a tangle, her T-shirt half way up her slender back, and arms and legs clutching the tree branch for dear life. 'Get me down. It's going to kill me!' She screamed again, then shut her eyes and adopted a face like she'd watched a horror film in the dark in a creepy house on her own, then discovered red-eyed spiders watching her too.

At that moment Dornoch flicked up a bulky black bag that lay in the garden. He tossed it, but the bag caught on his horns so he tussled with it, head-butting and shaking. The bag ripped and spewed its multicoloured contents across the hummocky lawn of Flora's Highlands home.

'Your bag?' Hamish said.

'No, the beast from the abyss brought luggage. Of course it's my bag. And he's probably smashed my phone and camera!'

Hamish wished he had his own phone to take pics. This could go viral.

'You have to calm down.'

Callie peeked with one opened eye and screamed afresh.

Hamish took in a laboured breath. Why the hell had he fallen so hard for a woman more tied up than a knots convention? 'It's the screaming that's enraging him, Callie. Enough already.'

Watching her struggle in anger, he was reminded of Callie aged fifteen. When out on a country walk, she'd had her walking boot sucked off by a cowpat and spent the entire way hopping back with him as her aide, ranting like a crazy thing. He remembered he'd so wanted to kiss her even back then.

'How can I stay calm when I'm about to fall to my death and become a human haggis?'

'He'll settle if you stop screaming. I know this ram. He comes here to eat; he's old and grumpy, but usually stable. I know how he feels.'

She could do with a healthy dose of stable herself. She hung upside down and he was talking to her half-bared back — attractive back that it was. His eyes stayed on her neat behind and strong legs that kept her aloft. The tight jeans did everything for her. He'd like to replay this moment in his memory. Her hair was a shock of platinum dandelion fluff. Callie Dewar was more attractive yet when ruffled and indisposed.

He figured this was payback for all her café back-off vibes. Maybe he should let her suffer for longer? But he couldn't bring himself to be mean to his Callie Dewar.

He could smell the wet grass from the divots of turf Dornoch had lifted with his angry hooves. But suddenly the crazed ram lost interest and calmed after the rucksack incident. His attention switched from Callie to chewing her spotted pyjama trousers like they were a new delicacy with piquant appeal. He stopped and stared at the tree before emitting an appreciative baa.

'Hope they weren't treasured mementos. You might have to pump his stomach.' Hamish stifled a grin; he'd sort Dornoch. But he'd also like to do bad things to his elderly aunt and sister. Had they sent Callie here on purpose to drive him nuts, or cause the biggest fight the region had ever seen? They were the only ones who knew his whereabouts. She'd travelled a long way to come to apologise for kicking him out.

'Before I help, I want one question answered. What are you doing here, Callie?'

'Enjoying the view. Don't ask stupid questions!' She screamed, now irate. 'What are *you* doing, life-modelling in ladies' nightwear? Help me.'

Hamish remembered his virtually-naked-but-for-a-robe state, and embarrassment clenched in his gut. He was one towel-fabric knot away from eternal mortification. 'I didn't know you could get so cross.'

'I have an aversion to sheep. This is my nightmare situation.'

The ram dropped his snack remains,

looked up at Callie again, then snorted, and she screamed at high volume. Bored with eating, he ran at the tree full-tilt again. Perhaps it had been an energising pit-stop. His behaviour suggested sound was his trigger, so maybe Callie had got her just deserts by not listening.

'Give me ten seconds — I'll be back, and stop screaming,' Hamish yelled. He had to get out of the terry robe before his male pride totally disintegrated.

'But I can't hold on much longer . . . I'm not kidding.'

Hamish ran to fetch a coat, hastily don some jeans, and grab the shepherd's crook and feedbag in the boot-room, since Dornoch was a sucker for oats. Moments later he ran back in wellingtons, a zipped-up wax jacket covering his still-bare chest.

Dornoch turned, smelled the pungent feed on the breeze, and with a long sheep-style whinny let out a shaky breath. His nostrils flared, but the crazy-eyed state dissipated.

'Dornoch, come get something nice.'

Hamish pushed the betraying attraction he felt away. Callie was a no-go zone. At least she'd stopped screaming. Then he twigged that she was crying, and the sound speared his gut.

'Don't cry. Be strong. We still have to get you down from there,' he urged her. As the ram chowed down, Hamish gently coaxed the animal to follow him out of the garden with calming words and a line of feed. It took a few minutes of nudging, but he got there, and managed to close the gate. Dornoch stood nibbling his reward as if he hadn't been AWOL moments before.

Hamish ran to the tree and threw the crook down. Then he sighed and braced himself; he hoped he could get through this and weather having Callie here and up close in his arms. Like he had a choice. Not.

'Let go — I'll catch you. I won't let you fall. I'm ready — drop down on me,' he urged.

With a squeal, Callie landed in his arms.

'The things you'll do to get my attention,' he quipped, but his joke was ill-timed; especially with her nuzzling against his chest, so that his hands naturally fell onto her warm curves. When their gazes met, he appreciated how much she affected him when she burst into fresh tears.

'Callie, don't cry. It's only an old sheep messing you about for kicks. It gets boring in the Highlands, so they like to play with the tourists for entertainment. It could've happened to anybody. You're safe now. Dinny fash, lass.'

'I hate sheep. I had a bad accident with one, and ever since I run the other way. Why does everything I touch go wrong lately?'

'Maybe you should open up and tell me about it, instead of pushing everybody out.' Something in Hamish quaked at her reaction — the sad eyes, her pale face, her trembling in his arms, and fresh tears running down her alabaster skin. And he was lost. He'd been there before. It transported him back over a decade to her eyes misting with hurt after he'd made the biggest prat of himself by faking a stop to their walk on the physical side. When he'd woken up to the truth too late — that he couldn't encourage her crush on him, then waltz back off to law school and leave her — he'd had to do the brave thing and stop things for her sake.

'Please don't cry,' he said hoarsely.

She covered her face with her hands and cosied into him. And immediately he was turned on as well as appalled at his primal response to this woman. His desire had woken up and wanted action. He was holding the hottest woman he knew in his arms, so close and tempting. Dornoch wasn't the only one in a state.

Callie looked at him, eyes sparkling like blue topaz behind tears. 'Why did you have to be here?'

'Why did you have to come here to drive me crazy?' he replied.

'Flora tricked us,' she answered with shaky breaths. 'But I'm too tired to fight.'

Hamish set her on her feet and steadied her with firm hands, noticing that they were nearer than they'd been in years. 'We're here together alone. We're not going to fight, are we?'

'I wouldn't have survived the sheep if you hadn't been here. Thank you.' Callie watched him, then shrugged her shoulders. Shoulders that were slender and waiflike now that she had no café to command or chef's coat to hide under. And for once she wasn't pushing him away or making rude comments. For once he wasn't the one in the wrong.

'Glad I could help,' he answered, and found he was watching her lips, itching to touch them with his thumb. Or his mouth.

'Never had you down as the gallant knight type.'

'Maybe you only had to ask.' Hamish recognised the flare of desire in her gaze. He could hear her breathing and feel the anxious frustration seep from her.

'Callie, you've no idea what you do to me. I'm not joking about that.' He pulled her body into alignment with his. Complete mistake — but his body and mind didn't care.

Before he knew it, he tugged her into his arms. Being up close and finally alone fired his deep regard for this amazing woman. 'You have no idea how much I care about you.'

Her fragility was magnified, her defences and bluster erased. For once they were man and woman forced to interact. Under normal circumstances he'd nix his urge for contact; but now his fingers touched her chin, then he slanted his head and claimed her lips, as he'd longed to do. 'What can be so bad we can't get around it together?'

'Sometimes talking is the worst thing to do,' Callie responded. Her mouth opened under his and her tongue tentatively accepted his.

She was as sweet as Madeira wine and the finest petit fours all at the same time. And he craved the feast of her. Adrenaline and deep yearning spiked and grand prix raced for supremacy inside him. 'I'm hooked on you, Cal.'

She whispered, 'I've been hung up on you for too many years of my life.'

He clutched her close and kissed her again. Callie Dewar was a temptation tornado beneath the bluster. And he found he loved it even more than he'd ever imagined. Hamish knew he was probably crazy to crank their chaos regardless of consequences, but Callie's confidences urged him not to care. She in turn tugged him close, and their pounding heartbeats merged. How had they got their wires crossed for so long?

'Ever think maybe my sister and aunt might be on to something by forcing us together?' he said. 'We've made more progress in the last ten minutes than ever before.'

'I'd disagree with you. But you're the lawyer who wins all the arguments.'

He grinned and enjoyed their proximity. 'So stop talking and just kiss me back.' He kissed her because resistance was futile. And he'd wanted to do this ever since forever was invented.

5

'It's going to rain. Let's go inside,' Hamish told her.

Callie saw that in her state of ram-induced disarray, she'd lost a running shoe. She was so caught up in looking at her mismatched feet that she didn't notice Hamish had the missing trainer in his hand. Like Prince Charming turned multi-tasker, he knelt down to replace it.

The rain began to fall around them as they reached the cottage's back door. Her breathing still hadn't calmed, and her head was in more of a mess than her bag's contents.

What should she do now? Scram? Demand Hamish relinquish the cottage? Go back on her crazy kiss confidences? But what would be the point? It was going to rain and her campervan was stranded. Hamish beckoned with his head for her to follow through into Bracken Cottage.

She drew in a shocked breath, her first deep inhalation in what seemed a lifetime, noticing that the 'cottage' wasn't any kind she'd ever known — it was palatial. It had old Scots 'country house' charm and even a turret, plus two storeys and windows that suggested capacity for many guests. She stood taking in the wide wooden staircase, the hall with expansive rafters, and the stained-glass window in a medley of startling hues.

'This place is more a hotel than a cottage,' Callie commented. Then she realised she was alone and Hamish had vanished. A door clicked nearby, and she noticed him return as she ogled Flora's place. He looked more himself in jeans and the shirt. Bathrobes would, in future, bring 'Hamish indisposed' memories by default.

'I believe it used to be a hunting lodge,' Hamish told her.

'Makes sense. It's big enough.'

The rain drummed in earnest, rattling hard on the roof as Hamish shut the windows tight. Shivering, Callie found herself wondering where the ram would shelter.

Hamish walked past the staircase made for making grand entrances to a door that led to a kitchen. He told her, 'Let's get a drink. I think we both need one.'

Callie gulped back her trepidation. She took her key out of her pocket, glad she'd stowed it safely there and not in her ravaged bag. 'I guess I should give you this, since you claimed the place first.'

Hamish stared hard. 'Don't be silly. My aunt invited you to come here. You have equal rights to it.'

'She told me this would be the perfect escape, a week's complimentary stay. Only now I see it has a surprise condition attached. Does she specialise in reconciliations?'

Hamish walked ahead into a vast wood-beamed kitchen so huge it could grace an abbey full of monks. 'I'm sensing more of a set-up than a mix-up.

My aunt has answering to do. Of course, you'll stay. There's no question of you leaving.'

At least with a lot of rooms she'd have space to regroup; pull her sensible brain cells together and fill him in that they really should never entertain trying to rebuild past bridges that had long crumbled underfoot. Then Callie remembered that Dornoch the rampaging behemoth was probably waiting somewhere outside, and she felt grateful she had Hamish's company.

She informed him on a rushed breath, 'I don't fancy facing Dornoch again, and I'm not ready to move on tonight. No campervan. It broke down en route.'

'I'll make sure the gate's securely locked while you're here, and help you get the van relayed,' he answered. He motioned to a central island with stools for her to sit down.

They both looked at the window as blinding lightening flashed. 'Some storm,' Hamish remarked.

'Some place.' Callie let herself take in the interior. The ceilings were vast. The layout was magazine-photo-shoot-ready. The rustic bespoke wood was drool-worthy, and Callie found herself coveting the décor. 'Your aunt never does things by halves.'

'Runs in the family.' Hamish gave a jokey grin, until thunder clattered, making Callie jump out of her skin. 'You okay? Sit down and relax,' he urged, and Callie was glad to slide onto a wooden stool.

The kitchen middle island was an expanse of wood, and the burnished-steel oven had more burners and grills than could cater for a feast after battle. Modern bi-fold glass doors showcased lush green hills and fields being drenched by the hard-falling rain. This might be Highland living, but mod cons abounded. Rough-hewn quarry tiles in all areas made her drawn to explore more of it. Again lightening flashed, drawing Callie up sharp.

'It's fabulous,' she whispered, 'but I

don't think I'd have liked being here all alone.' Even if she had to share it with Hamish until she fathomed an escape plan, she'd manage.

'What would you have done? Slept up a tree? Forget about it now. I'll find you a drink.' Hamish fixed her with a level stare. She felt like he could X-ray her right to the emotions that ran through her. 'I'd no idea you had such tree-scaling talents. I remember climbing with you once, though I was about ten at the time.'

'A lifetime ago,' she answered just as deafening thunder banged harder than ever like warring guns above them. If she'd thought the sheep attack had been frightening, this Highland storm might take the prize.

Sensing her fear, Hamish came towards her and smoothed his hands down her arms, making her shiver. The weather matched the turmoil inside her, alone here with Hamish. Her mind kept returning to his earlier confessions that he had lingering feelings for her, and she found she couldn't ignore the new knowledge. How had she missed those signals for so long?

'Tea? Something stronger?' he asked.

'Something strong. The thunder is freaking me out.'

Then she wondered . . . was drinking near Hamish Gordon wise? But he'd already returned with whisky in one hand and wine in the other. The sight of Merlot won hands down.

The satisfying glug of the liquid filling the crystal glass soothed Callie's nerves. His handsome face set in concentration somehow made him more kissable than ever. Now she admitted she shared her customers' infatuations, but she had first-hand knowledge of what his lips could inspire. That kiss outside. Wow.

'The kiss was a mistake,' she voiced.

'For you, maybe. Not for me.'

Feeling the need to get it dealt with, she repeated, 'We can't. Heat of the moment. We were both in a heightened state.'

Hamish's gaze drilled hers. 'That right?'

'Trauma response.'

'I've never had my kisses described like that before. I'd take it as a compliment, but I'm sure it's not going the way I want it to.' He paused, and the rain continued to pelt down. They could hear its lively relentless percussion beat adding an extra dimension to their words.

Callie licked her lips. 'You have comforting arms. But we really don't need to go over old ground. Our shared history wouldn't recommend it.'

Hamish handed her a glass, and she was mortified to see her fingers shake.

He kept his gaze firmly rooted to hers. 'For me, our kiss was no mistake. Call it a long-hidden ambition realised. Because I like you a lot, yet you always push me away.'

Sure, he'd pressed her destiny-revisited button and activated hope. He'd admitted to attraction and kissed her like he meant it. But could she really let one amazing kiss reset all her coping parameters? Wouldn't the desire he stirred only lead to more heartache? Her thoughts tumbled like light dough in a mixer set on high speed. Given her current problems, did she even know what kind of future she wanted? Confronting her past was not on the list.

Outside the large windows, the lightening flashed like a million paparazzi unleashed. Just like Hamish was blinding her with his revelations. 'It's getting worse,' she said.

'Us or the storm?'

She answered, 'All of it. Sorry if I led you on. It's a nice idea, but it can't ever go anywhere. I mean that.'

The thunder last time had nothing on this dramatic rumble of doom above them that stretched on like a war cry from the gods. The hurt Callie saw on Hamish's face caused a conscience struggle inside her. Was he telling the truth? Could she trust his words? And even if he was, could she really be what Hamish wanted?

He didn't meet her gaze, but his face told of dark disappointment. 'I read the situation wrong.'

'We can see past it. We're old friends.'

'St. Andrews didn't feel remotely friendly to me.'

Callie sipped, feeling the warming liquid burn a steady path down into her stomach. Her heart lightened, and she breathed easier as some of her tension unfurled and a new bravery took hold. She laid the glass down. 'I think together on any level, we don't work.'

'You know what I think,' he said, breathing deeply and standing tall before her. So tall she had to look up as if scanning a mountain peak. Harder to master than Ben Nevis. And he was just as majestic and daunting when in true lawyer debate mode. 'I think *you* struggle. You're in denial because you have issues. I think you're frightened to open up and share your load, and you hide. You tuck your fear deep with bristling anger. All I really want to do is help you because I care. And I want to break through your tough shell.' His jaw flexed, and something inside her trembled seeing it. Handsome on the outside, but speaking from integrity.

Outside, the rain had changed in pitch. It was lighter. Still falling hard, but the pace of the storm had eased. All had changed around them.

Callie reeled because Hamish always got straight to the heart of the issue, even when she struggled to conceal it, and that took her breath away. He made her feel so transparent. 'You mean it don't you?' she said.

'I'm not into throwaway lines. Or false claims.'

He acted like he knew what she needed better than she did. Did he? She gulped against a dry throat. He was more of a threat, a force to be reckoned with, than she liked. His so ably rumbling her wrecked her emotionally and collapsed her fake control. Tears began falling softly. She blinked on fast speed like car wind-screen wipers set to the max.

He closed in the space and enfolded her hands into his. 'Upsetting you is the last thing I want.' He tugged her close.

'I want you to realise I care.' He linked fingers with hers with one hand while the other wrapped around her shoulder, rubbing her skin and soothing. His touch made her want to melt into a puddle of surrender to the pain; to disclose the real root of her sorrow. But she really couldn't go there. Hamish was most possibly the last person she'd ever want to have to experience that.

'What's wrong?' he asked her. 'You're hurting. Give me a window on this to help you, Cal.'

And that's when she knew. She didn't just have a crush on him. She loved him. Everything. The whole package of Hamish Gordon: lawyer, friend and man. 'You really want your holiday spoiled with sob stories?'

The rain eased. What had been a full-scale drain-dumping flood was now just the pattering end of a deluge. The flood had eased and the cloud-dumping abated while the drains struggled with the aftermath.

'I'm a good listener,' he said. 'Believe

it or not, it's the most important part of my job.'

'Then I think you'll need a seat and a double measure to drink.'

★ ★ ★

'You're right. I'm having a crisis.' Callie let her gaze hold his. Her vulnerable heart throbbed tight, tender. Relief tangled with fear inside her, making her breaths short. She'd been mixed up too long; never having the courage to confide brought diminished inner peace. An instinct pulled her to backtrack and renege, but she pushed against it. She needed this release like gulps of air during a flat-out swim.

' 'Crisis' is a very strong word,' Hamish said, his voice a deep caress. 'Nobody's died. Everything can be solved if we're calm and rational and we tease our problems apart.'

But he didn't know the half of it. Her fertility bombshell hurt too much to share. She couldn't take his compassion or his pity. She steadied her hands on the table. 'Something has to change before my life implodes.' Her voice croaked, perhaps caused by the confusion racing around inside her.

'You're shaking.' He drew his chair nearer so he was close, without touching.

'I need to leave the business. I've lost the love. It's a burden that's dragging me lower with every passing month. And other things have changed.'

'Are you in trouble financially?'

'No.' She shook her head. 'It's no cash cow, but I get by. The café does okay, but it saps my energies. I have to throw everything I have into the business. I work around the clock. I'm so squashed by my grandfather's legacy that I've forgotten what I want. Who I am.' She finally let it out in a long, slow exhale.

'If that's how you feel, then you know the answer already. You need to let it go.'

'But . . . Grandpa worked to make that footprint of his own, and I'm set to

106

wave it all goodbye.'

'You've worked too hard on some-body else's dream already.'

'That doesn't excuse it, Hamish.'

Sitting close and watching her with those sombre eyes, he made her heart zoom and magnetised her to overload. His calm sense, intelligent approach and passion emanated from every pore. She breathed in pine and citrus, his scent, like a perfect woodland walk in sunshine. Her pulse slowed.

'You can do this, Cal. Just because you're making the decision alone doesn't make it wrong.'

'But you're the brave career go-getter. I'm Callie the baker who's always worked in one place.'

'Have you considered recruiting a manager to enable you to step away stage by stage?'

'You know what I'm like. I'd come back to the café and start involving myself.' Callie shrugged, glad to be able to finally vent her true concerns.

Hamish reached out for her hand.

'Yes I do know. Controlling. Bossy. Detail-obsessed. But that's what makes you brilliant. But if it doesn't give you joy, why continue? You just need a hand to hold, a friend.'

She pushed her tongue to the roof of her mouth. 'I don't deserve this. I sacked you. You really, really shouldn't be this nice to me.'

Hamish grinned ruefully. 'I happen to think we could use this time to sort our lives out. You're not the only one at a crossroads.'

She stared hard at him. She'd never really explored the true reasons behind his return. 'I thought you were kidding about leaving Strasbourg.'

'Ever wake up and realise you've got everything you worked for and ever wanted, and it's not half as inspiring as you'd imagined it would be?'

'Actually, I've never had a chance to dream at all.'

'Then use this chance to feed your soul, Callie. You need this break. I'll help you figure it out.'

For once he might just be right. Callie forced a smile and hoped she was up to withstanding it. But she was too tired to fight. She did need soul coaching, and more than anything she needed a break. She itched to tell him about her other problem, but the pain that squeezed her heart stopped her.

She smiled tentatively. 'I think I can say yes to that.'

★　★　★

The doorbell rang, breaking the spell, and both Callie and Hamish started in surprise. 'Nobody knows I'm here,' Hamish remarked. 'Who can it possibly be?'

'Maybe the ram is back for a rematch and has brought his big brother.'

He shook his head. 'I hope not. My ears are still ringing from the earlier screaming.' He stood. 'I'll be back shortly.' Hamish strode from the room. His commanding yet reassuring presence left a void when he exited.

Callie had a sudden itch to flee the enormity of what she was facing. She'd confided too much. Hamish was being the nice guy. Remaining here left her vulnerable — and what if she broke down completely? The cottage might be a lovely hideaway; but being totally honest, wasn't she kidding herself thinking she could resist him? His compassion and kind words melted weak spots in her. Was her unresolved emotional maelstrom a good reason to chum with the man who still affected her? Perhaps she'd been too hasty saying yes.

Hamish's greeting and the visitor's response pulled her from her thoughts. She could hear the conversation from the hallway clearly because of the echo effect of the quarry tiles.

'I'm Agnes Drysdale, a friend of your Aunt Flora's from the croft at Rowan Byres.'

'I'm Hamish. It's been a few years since we last saw each other.'

'You were naught but a lad.' Compared to Hamish's deep surly rumble, the unseen female's voice lilted like a twittering bird. 'I've brought dinner. May I set up the dining room now?'

'Thank you; very kind,' he gruffly muttered.

'I'll set up as arranged with Flora. I'll be as quiet as a mouse; you won't know I'm here. I did promise I'd lay out the meal to her instructions. She said you'd have company.'

Callie listened, holding her breath. What had Flora done? She was determined to ignore the gremlin doubts that told her Hamish had been as much in the dark as she had. Of course she could trust that he was as bamboozled as she was by Flora's arrangements. This hadn't been a Gordon family plan to trap her, surely?

She peeked through the door-hinge crack. Her heart tattooed a drum-pace in her chest when the recognition crashed-landed that her hair must be a haystack after the tree escapade. She must look like a woman from the wildest wood. Hamish could never in a million years find her appealing like this.

Squinting through the door crack, she saw Agnes's shock of white curled hair and pair of stout shoes, tweed skirt, jumper and padded jacket. She had some sort of trolley affair covered in domed plates, and they both moved as Callie dived behind the door as the trolley passed. As waitresses went, this little Highland lady presented a quirky surprise.

'And is the lassie okay now?' Agnes asked.

'Who?' Hamish answered.

'The pretty lass in the lilac T-shirt. The one who arrived earlier. My Alec saw her running from the daft sheep. By the time he got here to help, you had things in hand — as if Dornoch would do anything to a soul anyway. That daftie would lick her to death. Of course, high-pitched noises are quite another thing. He nearly took Alec's leg off when he practised his bagpipes at the end of the field. Is she all right?'

'Rest assured, no harm done.'

'Brought your lass here to romance her in the glens? You'll not find a better spot for inspiring affection. Thinking of a proposal?'

Hamish cleared his throat. 'She's a colleague, and is lying down at the moment. The incident shook her.'

The woman's tone was loaded with meaning. 'Lying down, eh? Lucky lassie. Tell her the sheep aren't usually hostile hereabouts. Wouldn't want her getting a bad impression.'

Callie stood holding her breath, imagining Hamish's jaw doing clench aerobics. Her heart thumped fast and her mouth had gone dry.

'Next time, give him turnips. The beast is tumshie mad. He'll eat from her hand then. Friend for life.'

Callie shuddered. There was no way another run-in with that horned pyjama-eater was ever happening. Not that she'd stick around here for longer than necessary after the mayhem she'd unleashed. If she could only get Violet back into action and drive back home to rest, away from all the challenges and surprises. So much for a scenic holiday.

Agnes continued waxing lyrical in her quirky accent. 'She's lucky Dornoch's girlfriend Doris wasn't here — she's the nasty piece. Lucky the lass had a tree to hide in, too. I hope it hasn't fair put her off her dinner. It's a choice of spiced lamb or vegetarian haggis. Soup for starter, cranachan for afters. Mints, coffee, whiskies and liqueurs. Just as we serve our hotel guests; the ones on exclusive tariff.'

Hamish's voice took a brusque edge as he and Agnes went back down the hallway. 'I'll pass on your tips. I'm sure she'll be fine once she's had a meal, and thank you for dinner.'

'Aye, lad. Nice to be involved in planning for this wee romantic reunion.'

'As I said, we're working on a project. What can I give you for payment?'

'Not a thing. This is your aunt's gift. Have a wonderful night.'

The door shut after a flurry of

Scots-burr-laden thanks and goodbyes. Callie's pulse hammered and she was glad their visitor had finally gone.

But Hamish's tone told her fresh danger lurked. 'The dinner plans confirm my aunt knew she'd sent us both here on purpose. Should we feel manipulated? Or take the hint that we have talking to do?'

His eyes stayed on her, staring hard, waiting for an answer she felt ill-equipped to give. She resented being thrust into this, and yet inside she still felt magnetised by the man.

'Whatever you decide, I want you to stay. I want you to stay more than you know. Say you will?'

Hell. Wasn't it bad enough she'd steeled herself against him? Bad enough her life was in a mess and her hopes were on the rocks? She might never have a family. How could she ever hope to straighten herself out with Hamish here? But there was no way she was talking about babies she would never have with the man who held her heart in the palm of his hand. A man she'd had a crush on for way too long.

'I'll agree to think about it. But let's not let the dinner go to waste.' Callie kept her nerves on tight rein. 'Once I straighten myself up, I'll join you to eat. Hungry work, this ram-dodging and tree-climbing.'

Hamish smiled. 'Bathroom is at the top of the stairs — towels in the closet. My aunt has a wardrobe full of clothes. I'll go and find something you can wear. Prepare yourself for dining dressed in tartan or tweed tonight.'

Callie groaned. 'And I was almost looking forward to it. Tartan is so not my look.'

'You, my dear Callie, look sensational even hanging from a tree. Your clothes aren't what catch my attention. So I'm positive you'll rock any look. Meet me for our dinner with destiny when you're ready.' His eyes lit like burning embers, and fired her inside more than any dram.

6

A stretchy black skirt and a silky sapphire blouse in Flora's closet of a hundred plaids helped Hamish save the day as a stylist. Teamed with her flat pumps and newly washed hair, Callie felt almost normal when she emerged after changing.

'I'm back,' she called softly when she found the kitchen empty.

'In here,' Hamish called to her from a room down the hallway. 'All set for dinner. Hope you're hungry. There's masses. It would feed a horde.'

'You aren't kidding either!'

Bracken Croft's dining room boasted a vast and gleaming dark wood table set with silverware, crystal goblets and a fire crackling in a fine stone hearth. The *Downton Abbey* cast would not have been disappointed by the trappings or the sublime Highlands vista. Callie let her gaze rove across Flora's home. The farmhouse rolled out at its exterior into a modern architect's dream extension. She'd known money wasn't an issue for Flora, but hadn't quite appreciated how loaded she was.

'Now I see why Flora fell for this place,' said Callie. 'Tranquil perfection.' Though it was the man beside her that really had her feeling giddy and impressed. He wore smart-casual too well and her heart revved in her chest. His smile could part the thickest clouds and flood the greyest skies. Hamish nursed a whisky, though she knew he rarely drank. He'd changed into smart trousers and a fresh grey polo shirt.

'You look great,' he told her.

He looked better. Way better. 'Thanks. I must ask Flora if we can swap clothes in future.' She grinned. 'Though I'm not sure that when she lent me the keys, she pictured me stealing her fashions.' Callie motioned to the long table before them. 'Sure beats takeaway.'

A silver gas food burner kept their

tureens of dinner piping hot. Even fragrant lit candles were set in a silver candelabra. Hamish stood nearby with a bottle in one hand, empty glass in another. Callie had never been a whisky drinker. The script on the bottle looked impressive as he poured her a glass without asking. She figured it was non-negotiable.

Hamish swigged and Callie commented, 'I've never seen you drink before.'

'Maybe I'm nervous.'

'Why ever would you be nervous around me?'

'You really have to ask?' He sat the glass down. 'I don't usually, but I'm on holiday. Figured I deserve some Dutch courage.'

Her fingers shook as she took the crystal glass he'd left for her. The smell of his lemon soap on her skin gave her a wild thrill, as did the touch of their fingertips.

Hamish took her by surprise when he said, 'So Flora is playing match-maker?'

'Flora is complex. Underhanded, yet prim and proper, and thoroughly well-versed in skulduggery. She could be a pirate.'

'I think she and Linley need a strong talking-to. My sister is just as bad as my aunt. She's been hinting at the opportunity for us to get together. She goes on and on and on.'

'Don't worry, I'll be out of your hair as soon as I can book a hotel room tomorrow.'

Hamish's gaze accused her. 'I don't plan to turn you out. I'm happy you're here.' He raised an eyebrow and placed his glass firmly on the mantel. 'There's plenty of space for both of us. Where's your van? What happened to it? You didn't have an accident?' His voice hitched.

'Engine trouble. A pub barman I met took pity on me and says he'll fix it. Serves me right for not putting her in for a full service before I left.'

'You let a stranger drive you here?' Hamish's face became suddenly dark and angry. Unfortunately she felt like

Hamish was taking charge of her failings and she'd just been promoted to his priority case.

'It's fine. He's promised to fix the van.'

'Lucky for you. But a lone woman should never take such risks.'

'Are you lecturing me, Hamish?'

'I'm not keen on some stranger taking on such a job without references.' He pushed his hand through his hair then pursed his lips, his eyes scrutinising the table before him as he mentally worried at her choices. 'What do you know about him? Could be a cowboy. I'd really prefer to find a reputable mechanic myself. If you'll agree?'

'Thank you, but it's in hand.' Callie sipped, then winced at the whisky's taste. 'Do people honestly drink this? It's just not for me.'

Hamish turned to stand right before her. 'Let's eat. And once we've had dinner, I have a proposal. And this one is as serious as it gets. It's been a long time coming.'

★ ★ ★

They ate in silence but for occasional small talk. Callie was hungry, and she'd been given a sumptuous feast, so even nerves and worries about being set up with Hamish couldn't get in the way of her appetite. But her mind obsessed over his words. And the wine didn't taste as good as it should when she had so many thoughts jostling. This was exactly the kind of thing that made her think leaving would've been wise.

Before she knew it, they'd finished their cranachan desserts — tart raspberries and oats in a creamy whisky-kick trifle — and Hamish sat staring at Callie from the other end of the table. 'I have something I'd like to say,' he announced, and then circled the table and pulled her hand into his as he knelt at her feet. 'I want us to be together. That's as simple as it gets.'

Callie blinked at him but didn't answer. 'You're not serious?'

His eyes danced, underlining his

fervour. 'Completely. I want a relationship with you. I'm not going back to Strasbourg. I'm not bailing on us or letting you block me out any longer.'

At one time she'd have yearned for such words and done joyful cartwheels. But she didn't want Hamish's self-sacrifice or logic Band-Aids to her plight. He couldn't just charge in with plans, no matter how much he wanted to help.

'No, Hamish. The crazy thing is, you mean it. I think that heat-of-the-moment thing outside should make us both take a step back. You pushed me away once before, remember?'

She heard him suck in a breath. 'Don't remind me of what a daft idiot I was as a teenager. I kissed you and pushed you away like a fool. But it was because you were worth more than a quick fling, Cal. I knew me leaving for law school would mess with your head, and I knew you'd stick with the café. It hurt me doing that, but it hurt you too; I've forever regretted that.'

'Oh.' She slowly digested his answer. 'I just thought I turned you off.'

'You can't even imagine how wrong that statement is. I never should have walked away the first time.' To underline the words, he rubbed the backs of her hands. 'You need someone to unburden to. Someone who'll listen and guide you. I want to be there. And if love can blossom from that, then all the better.'

He'd no idea how close he was to the turmoil within her. Not only with the café, but also her shattered life and health challenges. Her family future black hole. Her failures in every area of her life. She did need what he was offering, but she wasn't ready yet.

His jaw flexed resolute and he reached to tug her close. Callie could feel his warm breath against the skin of her cheek. He took a strand of her hair between his fingers. 'Trust me. I'll never let you down again. And I'm not going anywhere. You mess with my good sense and I'm addicted.' Hamish kissed her cheek; the move made her gasp as his mouth slid over hers, communicating the fervour of his need like no words could.

Her bones melted and her insides electrified. She felt like she'd waited her whole life for this moment, and it more than measured up to her dreams. But she knew the Gordons full well. It might all look rosy now, but sooner or later he'd want a family of his own. However she may kid herself, this was getting too deep, too fast.

She said in a rushed breath, 'I'll camp in Violet. I can't do this again with you. I don't doubt you, but it's me, not you.'

As if slapped, Hamish's gaze rebuked her. Then his jaw clenched, and his gaze bored into hers with licks of flame from the fire in the grate reflecting in glowing streaks. 'What more can I do to make you realise that I was young and a stupid fool, and I've regretted that night ever since? You're at liberty to leave any time, but I really don't want you to.'

His arms circled her waist keeping her captive. And something responded deep down in her heart. She knew she should be sensible. 'I came back to Scotland because I intended to give up everything. But it was clear you couldn't stand me. I've wanted you longer and more than I've ever wanted anything in my life.'

But how could he tell her these things when she'd had to bear news about him that had stung her hard? 'You were engaged. How can you tell me these things now?'

'I dated a girl but we were never engaged,' he said. 'Who told you that?'

'Linley.'

'She and my aunt interfere, and clearly have been working to their own agenda. You trust everything my aunt and sister do even after this? Why still run away from us, Cal?'

His lips met hers, and his kiss communicated the raw truth of all that he'd said. Callie watched him draw back slightly, then his hands cupped her face and he held her.

'What if you hurt me again?' she whispered.

'Let me prove I won't.'

He was so tempting. So bewitching. She wanted to step out of her life — the one that had so badly betrayed her. To live the dream and go with her heart. To pretend none of the things that were worrying her so much mattered. For these stolen hours, she was the Callie she wanted to be.

But wasn't that just a dream? She pulled back, wanting to seize the upper ground so badly it made her giddy. 'You can't twist me around your little finger again. Just because I'm in love with you doesn't mean . . . ' Callie blamed the mixology napalm of whisky and potent Merlot for the lapse. But blame didn't help when Hamish's gaze burned into hers.

'You love me?' he whispered.

Dark remorse whirled inside of her. She'd rather admit to a having a beehive in her pantry and radioactive ants in her kitchen. 'Want it typed up so I can sign it? Lawyer born and bred. I've liked you for way too long; tried to get over it. Nothing worked. But that doesn't mean I'm willing to get hurt again. We're not a great match, Hamish.'

'Callie, it's mutual. Feeling you slip from my fingers every time I tried to get close killed me. All I've ever wanted is you.' He held her with a firm embrace. 'I could never hurt you. I'll treat you with the greatest of care.'

She sucked in a breath. 'I want that. But I've nothing to offer you in return. So it's unfair to try, and I don't think we can have the kind of future you need.'

'Let me be the judge of that,' Hamish whispered, then kissed her.

Callie sensed he meant his words from the ardent passion she felt in him, and she responded with patent hunger. But deep inside she knew she was foolishly jeopardising her fragile, wary heart again.

★　★　★

They sat on the sofa before the roaring fire while dusk fell on the mountains outside, talking about past, present, hopes, fears. Hamish could read the wonder in Callie's eyes with every word. God knew he felt it too — the magic. He treasured that they'd opened up and let their love shine through. He was on a bigger high than winning his first court case.

'I can't believe we've avoided doing this all these years.' He smoothed a hand over her back, causing her to shiver. Then he gently pressed a kiss to her neck.

Callie's breathing hitched and she reminded herself not to melt into a puddle. 'I can. We're both stubborn.'

'Not stubborn.' He shook his head. 'Scared. This counted too much to let it go.'

'So what made you change your mind?' she asked.

'I want a family. I want to settle. I want a future with the woman I love.'

He saw the fear in her eyes and felt

her stiffen. 'Hey, not just yet. I'd quite like us to get to know each other and enjoy our new relationship first. Maybe we could share holidays. Some foreign travel together?'

'I'm not sure,' she answered, and he knew he'd freaked her out. Was he running too fast? He also figured she was very tired. It had been a long day of many surprises. 'Come on, Cinders. Time for bed.'

The panic on her face was all too clear this time.

'I didn't mean together. Don't worry, I'm not going to outstay my welcome. You can take the master suite. I'll use the downstairs guest room.' He rose and pulled her into his arms for another tender, careful kiss. He felt the tension ease after he'd kissed her and caressed her back. What worried her so? Why was she so easy to startle?

Callie shook her head. 'Don't be silly. You don't have to stay downstairs. I'll take the attic guest room. Fiona said she thought I'd like sleeping under the eaves.'

Hamish laughed. 'No go. The attic room is in use now. I'll show you if you like. There are things about me I might have to start confiding too. And now sounds like a good time to start.'

'Man of mystery, you're intriguing me now. Show me.' She nodded. He took her hand and pulled her after him to the central staircase, and then down a corridor that led to a door where another winding staircase lay. 'Come on then, Callie. Time to wake up and see there's more to me than you know. Maybe I'll surprise you.'

The bamboozled expression she wore after he threw open the door and she spotted his artwork told him all he needed to know. He released his breath.

'These are yours? You're a secret photographer? All this time and I never knew!'

His face heated with the attention. 'Yeah. Brought all my kit here figuring I'd get some great shots in my time off. I love it. It's not a hobby, it's a passion.'

'Don't let me stop you doing what

you came to do.'

'You can come with me if you like. I fancy some mountain landscapes. I want to go to some glens, weather permitting. Maybe try and get some local wildlife. We could take a picnic.'

'If ram shots are on the cards, count me out,' she laughed. And he pulled her closer for a hug. 'Though I'd quite like to see you in action, camera in hand, getting all arty on me.'

'It's birds that fascinate me. Maybe an otter or two if I'm lucky. I'm a keen birdwatcher. I've had a few commissions for my wildlife work.'

Callie was engrossed looking through an album of his shots, and his heart swelled to see her bright-eyed admiration. 'Wow, Hamish. I knew you were hot as a lawyer, but you're good at this too. As in really skilled. You could work in photography, you're that impressive.'

'It's a hobby that fascinates me, Cal. Just like you.' He kissed her cheek, and she grinned as she flicked through, admiring each photograph in turn.

'You know what I'm going to say, don't you?'

He tilted his head because he loved to kid her. 'That I'm a superhero, and you're not going to leave tomorrow now that you've seen my photographic talent?'

Callie pushed him in jest. 'I think if you really don't want to keep practising law, you already have other ideal avenues to pursue. I think you're way more talented than you let on.'

'The photography?' Hamish looked at her with an incredulous expression. 'No way. It's a hobby, pure and simple.'

'Hamish, you're way better than you think. And St. Andrews has lots of avenues for photographers. Weddings. Pro golf. Academia. You'd do well to think about that. Of course, maybe you just want to practise law in Fife.'

'Listen, law is what I do. It's what I know. Stepping outside of it would be a big undertaking.'

'So now you know how I feel. It's not all as easy as it sounds, is it?' She kissed his cheek ever so gently before handing him back his precious album. 'But maybe what you need to ask yourself is, is it really what you love?'

And right now he knew what he loved most. Callie. He guided her to the master suite, pleased she liked her bedroom. It was a hymn to minimalist décor in shades of white and grey with what must have been a super-king-sized bed. But the really impressive feature was the outstanding mountain back-drop view. She deserved this. He wanted her to feel looked-after.

'A lie-in is what the doctor orders for you,' he said, 'followed by an amazing cooked breakfast in bed delivered by yours truly.' Hamish lingered on the threshold, not wishing to make her feel intruded on. 'Like it?'

'It's beautiful.'

'Then I'll leave you. Help yourself to anything you need.'

'Thanks, Hamish. And thank you for today.'

'All part of the service.'

Hamish felt his heart beating at a crazy pace in his chest. Call it excitement for tomorrow to arrive, call it attraction; Callie was the cause of the live static zooming around his system.

'Goodnight. Sleep well,' she whispered.

'Tomorrow we'll talk again. We'll sort out how to proceed, Cal. It needn't be scary. I'll help if you confide and trust in me.'

'One-to-one conference with a lawyer? Sounds expensive. Don't think I can afford it.'

Hamish approached and kissed her lightly on the lips. 'For you — free. Pro bono and personal attention. Only I'm not here to be a lawyer — I'm here to make sure you never feel alone again.'

'I believe you mean that. For a lawyer, you're great at caring.'

'And just like with your cakes, when it comes to you I can't get enough.' Admitting his truths made Hamish's pulse quicken and sent thrills jiving inside him.

'Flattery will get you noticed. You're

full of surprises. Goodnight, Hamish.'

Dream of me, Callie. For I dream of you. And I hope that you might still love me back one day. 'Night, Cal. Sweet dreams. And trust they can come true.'

7

Callie woke to her new location, and after her initial surprise revelled in the feel of the sheets and the size of the bed. This was way better than any fancy hotel. She showered and headed downstairs for breakfast with a spring in her step, only to find Hamish already up, active and engrossed in creating a breakfast to rival their dinner feast for variety.

'Did you get up at dawn to prep for this?' she asked him. 'Are we expecting guests?'

'Only one VIP guest, and that's you.' His grin sent her insides round a helter-skelter of excitement.

'You do a mean line in flattery, Mr. Gordon. And if your breakfast is as good as your charm, we're on to a winner.' Callie knew she was good at bluffing calm-and-casual, when in reality her mouth had gone dry just watching him. He looked fresh and vital; strong and relaxed in his sweats and polo shirt. He neared her, then reached out to touch her arm.

'Sleep well? You look refreshed.'

'Like a baby. Flora has good taste in comfy beds and bed linens. I feel spoiled.'

'Sit down, and I'll tempt you with my creations. You're on holiday, and I figured prepping food was the last thing you needed.'

He was way too kind. Sun flooded in through the kitchen window, and the day held startling promise for walks and exploring. 'You planning on taking photographs today?' she asked.

'If you say you'll join me, I could be persuaded.'

'Only if it's what you planned. I don't want you changing your schedule because I'm here.'

'You're the most important part of my schedule. You need to start waking up to that, Callie.'

She smiled when he pulled out a chair for her. There were plates laid out with a traditional British breakfast, including toast with a choice of accompaniments. Callie went for eggs with tomatoes, started eating, and found she was ravenous even though she'd eaten well the night before. When Hamish widened his eyes at her appetite, she dabbed her lips with her napkin. 'Didn't you realise that I'm on the seafood diet? I see all this and I'm going to do my best to put a dent in it.'

'Your appetite suggests you've recovered from your Dornoch duel.' Hamish chuckled as he buttered his own hot toast.

'I actually haven't slept as well as I did last night in ages. I think it was my soul-searching. It's been therapeutic, and now I can't stop eating either. Maybe it's the Highland air.'

Hamish grinned. 'Ever consider that maybe I'm good for you?'

Callie inhaled, determined to avoid his significant inference; the words that made her belly flutter and her pulse pound faster. 'You've no idea of the weight that lifted when I got behind the wheel to come here and leave the daily grind behind. I'd lost sight of how much it drags me down. I'm sorry if I took that out on you back in St. Andrews.'

'Cal, no need to apologise. I'm only glad you've woken up to the fact that something needs to change. Why persist when it sucks the life from you? I mean that for your sake.'

She pushed her hand through her hair. 'Lots of reasons, and all of them good ones. The bakery goes way back, and Grandpa worked himself into the ground to succeed. Obligation, guilt, tradition, and the fact that I'm pretty good at my job. My customers love the café, and the thought of announcing that I may want to move on makes me shudder. I gave up dreams of college and stepped into the breach when I left high school. Dad left me without any choice, really.'

'You ever hear from your father?'

The F-word. Her father had long

stopped being that. He was now little short of a vagrant — except this one frequented Europe's scenic bays and harbours. A boho bum with more charm than money, Jimmy Dewar was her least popular relation. Even just his name had the power to chill her.

'My father turned his back on the family. Nearly broke the bank when he demanded his inheritance early from Gramps — all so he could live the high life on a sun-drenched yacht and play guitar. The ultimate midlife crisis. Wine and woman-chasing, more like.'

'I didn't realise he'd made financial demands. That must've cut the old man deep.'

'After Mum died Dad took it bad, Gramps told me years later. He hid his sorrows in the pub. His heart was never in raising me, or in the business either. So I could never leave Gramps to cope without help; he was the one who looked after me. And Gramps's other son, Uncle Bill, left home young; joined the navy in his teens and settled in New

Zealand. I really was the only one for him to pass the business to. So I didn't feel I had any right to decline it.'

'Misplaced guilt is no reason to stay. I get that your dad didn't want responsibility, and losing your mother left a huge void — but you're allowed the life you want.'

'If I stop, the struggle will have been for nothing.'

Hamish performed a smooth lawyer counter-move. 'I've noticed that you tell me what you think you should do. And you have strict rules, like you'd do something if you know it'll work out, even though nobody knows that before any venture. It's like you're doing things for others rather than for yourself. Everything is a risk; nobody would ever do anything otherwise. So what do you *want* to do, Cal?'

She sipped her tea, then sucked in a breath. She'd tucked her hopes too deep to find introspection easy, likely for fear of finding out she was either rubbish or the secret was a hopeless notion. And with the café always needing attention, it had been easier to hide behind the responsibility. She wanted most to strike out on her own, turning her hobby into a profession — but that was just a dream. Callie exhaled deeply and made her decision.

'Hand on heart, I most want to renovate old property; but failing that, I'm interested in interior design: refurbishing places with my own quirky twist, or having a showroom for bespoke interior pieces as a starting point. It fires me up like nothing else.' She gulped hard because it mattered that much admitting it. She'd never told a soul before.

The swift, soft touch of Hamish's lips on hers sent her heart bouncing in her chest, bubbles of delight popping inside her. 'You're a rare treasure, Callie Dewar,' he said. 'I knew you had hidden depths.'

She confided, 'I've a place out on the road to Ellie. It was a ramshackle barn when I bought it — holes in the roof and rats under the floorboards. Didn't have much money, but I have great gifted friends and traded services. A wedding cake here, a carpentry favour there. A few years later and it's pretty cool. Almost finished, actually.'

Hamish's gaze stayed on her — grey, questioning and revealing his surprise. 'I'm starting to see that you'd rather be sanding and stippling than caking and baking.'

Callie shrugged. 'I've learned pretty impressive skills with a soldering iron. I love wrought iron, and statement pieces like useable driftwood art. Doing that as my day job would be a dream come true. The café's great at times — but my creative side was never in patisserie.'

'Ever consider actually doing it? Selling up would help.'

'Profits haven't been appealing enough for anyone to be interested in buying.'

Hamish's face grew serious as he stilled his knife and fork and placed them on his plate. 'The café's lure may surprise you. A potential buyer may be easier to find than you think.'

'Maybe not in practice, Hamish. Though I like your optimism.'

He opened up a steel dish containing hot griddle cakes, then cut one in half for Callie to savour. 'Dig in. While you're chewing, have a think about this suggestion — what if I said I could find someone who'd buy your café and solve your problems in minimum time?'

She watched him, her eyes widening. 'You're kidding, surely.'

Hamish bit his food and rolled his eyes in pleasure. 'I'm serious. What if I said I could guarantee you a buyer at a premium price, to free you up to follow your heart? You could be following your dreams sooner than you think.'

'I'd say I'm interested, and I want to know more. Right now. Give me their number.'

He smiled widely, indicating he was feeling good about her enthusiasm. 'You're sitting beside the buyer this minute. I'll buy out your café, Callie. It's perfect for what I need. If you want to sell up, I'm interested. In fact I'll make you an offer right now.' And he went on to explain.

'Hamish, there's no way I can accept. And worse, I can see in your face you really think you mean it.' She felt her eyebrows knit as she pondered the ludicrous nature of what he'd just proposed. Though his words registered, her brain had assigned them to the empty rash-promises file. Blame her father, or the fact that she'd had to look out for herself and stay sceptical for so long. But Hamish really was just taking chivalry to extremes. This surely wasn't really going to happen.

'I'm serious,' Hamish told her, his eyes grave. 'Totally one hundred and ninety percent. I'll shake on it now.'

'Do you honestly want to buy a café? Lawyer to dishwasher? You'd be happy for about a month maximum, then you'd realise your mistake and have to put it up for sale all over again. Hamish, I can't see what's in it for you, other than a clientele that are utterly smitten by your charms.'

He watched her. 'There's office space upstairs. That's what I'm interested in. I'm thinking of establishing a practice in St. Andrews. Being a lawyer in my home town.'

'I hate to shatter your dreams, but the upstairs is dilapidated. It needs loads of money to refurbish. There's spider infestation, and birds' nests, and a patched-up hole in the tiles that I haven't had a chance to get fixed yet. That part of the building hasn't been in use since my grandfather's days.'

'I want my first business premises to be bespoke. Your building could offer the kind of blank canvas I need, and I'd probably renovate into the loft space to maximise potential.'

'What about the café? Would you just ditch it?'

'I'd find a chef and manager,' Hamish continued, his eyes sparkling as he listed the possibilities. 'Continue the kilted theme that's going so well. I see no need to dispose of a valuable asset, though I might like to add a private meeting room facility so that I can entertain clients or host meetings. Anyway, it'll be ideal for my morning macchiato. I'd be crazy to let that go.' And saying that, he slid his hand out to take Callie's. 'I have a hunch I'll find a backer, so it won't all be on my own. I have great connections.' He rose from his seat and moved to her side, then pulled her to her feet and put his hands around her shoulders, smoothing her T-shirt and making her head spin with the warm rush his touch induced.

'So here's my suggestion in full, Callie. I'm suggesting I give you the chance to follow those dreams you've hidden. But there's a condition attached — a makeover, since you're the expert. Think of our relationship as your first refurbishment project; taking you and me back to basics. What would your renovator side check for first?' His fingers played with her hair.

Callie wet her lips and gulped. 'I always do a survey. Check for solid structure. Keeper features . . . '

'We have all that and more, Cal. You and I offer solid promise. That's loads in our favour. Our portfolio together is pretty impressive. We're starting a hugely important relationship project that I want to last.'

And then the doorbell rang. Hamish went to answer and called, 'Callie, it's for you.'

She wasn't just surprised that anybody would call for her here; she was confused. When she saw the face at the door, disappointment slammed into her chest. Fraser from the pub at Ballachulish stood there, his head held slightly to the side as he regarded her, and his drawn eyebrows suggesting he hadn't expected she'd have male company.

'Fraser. Hi. How did you know where to find me?'

'Hi. You didn't think I'd really leave you stranded without checking you got back okay, lone lady and all? I made sure you got here before I left.'

Callie felt Hamish beside her — tall, commanding and a solid form with a slightly disapproving bristling vibe palpable in the air.

'Hope you don't mind me stopping by?' Fraser didn't look too worried. In fact, one foot was over the threshold as if he expected an invitation inside.

'This is an old friend from home, Hamish Gordon,' Callie introduced. 'Hamish, meet Fraser. He kindly brought me here yesterday and is taking care of the van.'

Hamish nodded, but made no move to shake hands or greet the other man. Callie figured it might be rude not to ask Fraser to come in. If he'd fixed Violet, then the least he deserved was her hospitality, even though something about this man didn't quite sit well. He'd followed her even though she'd thought he'd gone? Why hadn't he called first before arriving? He had her number. Why had he taken it upon himself to just turn up? Then again, as a bar manager he probably had limited free time. Maybe she was being too wary.

'Fancy a cup of tea?' she said finally,

seizing the initiative to banish the moody vibe between the men.

Fraser smiled. 'Thought you'd never ask. That's kind.'

Callie noticed the withdrawn and dark look on Hamish's face as he busied himself tidying the kitchen when they entered. She hoped she hadn't just bombed the day ahead. 'Take a seat. There's lots of food if you'd like breakfast.'

'No thanks,' Fraser said. 'I've already had something. We get a drayman delivery at five. I came to let you know I'll have to order parts for the van. It's going to take longer than I thought. Sorry, but it really can't be helped.'

'Oh. That's a shame. Thanks for coming all this way. You could have called me.'

'Actually, that's another reason I'm here,' said Fraser, putting his hand into his jacket pocket and withdrawing her mobile phone.

She hadn't even noticed it was gone, and now felt completely stupid and bad for suspecting the man for his actions.

'Oh my goodness. I hadn't noticed.'

'You left it at the pub. I figured it might be important, given you're here with no transport in a wilderness cottage. But I hadn't realised you'd have company. I can see I needn't have rushed.' He gave Hamish the kind of look Callie had seen Hamish already throw his way. There wasn't any love lost, and the dirty looks were being thrown like spears. She gathered patience, vowed to ignore them, and poured a cup from the teapot.

'That's so very kind of you,' she said. 'Help yourself to milk and sugar. Fortunately I'm not here alone, though it was a bit of a mix-up that's caused us to be here together. That wasn't in the plan. We have a double booking, but we know each other so it's all okay.' And why exactly she was explaining her accommodation issues to a man she barely knew, Callie had no idea.

'I have friends with a B and B if you need accommodation,' Fraser offered.

'It's fine. We'll manage here, but thanks.' The atmosphere dived as Fraser drank tea while Callie and Hamish flicked glances at him. She figured they'd rather battle on the lawn outside than partake in chit-chat.

Fraser slurped from his mug and perused the cottage. 'Nice place. Great décor.'

'Isn't it.'

'It's my aunt's cottage,' Hamish added softly.

'Then maybe you should do the gallant thing and give it up for the lady,' said Fraser.

Callie gulped. If she wasn't careful, there would be a fight on in Flora's kitchen, and she really didn't want to referee it. She rubbed her temples and started talking about the weather. When in doubt, use the British obsession with rainclouds and sunbursts to evade any discomfort.

'I have some calls to make.' Hamish balled up his tea towel and left the room, his shoulders broad and straight with pique.

'So, tell me exactly what's up with my campervan,' Callie said, hoping

Fraser wouldn't keep badgering her for a dinner date this time.

'Well . . . it's a very complex issue.'

As Callie tuned out, she hoped hard that she'd be able to get rid of Fraser in record time. She willed him to drink his tea down, finish his mechanics run-down, and get going to leave them in peace. She knew she'd have to work hard to get Hamish back onside.

⋆   ⋆   ⋆

Hamish heard the panic in his friend's voice when he answered his telephone call. Cameron Henderson was as level-headed and laid-back a man as you could find. So something must be bad to have him this worked up.

'I'm having a bit of a nightmare, Hamish. I'm really in a spot. I know it's a big ask, but could you help out?'

'What's happened? Nothing to do with Ginny and the baby, is it?'

'No, no. Baby will soon be here, God willing. I hate to come right out and boldly ask this, but can you come see us? I know it's an imposition to ask, but you're the best bloke I can think of in an entirely unique situation.'

Hamish was shocked, but Cameron was a good friend who would put himself out were their situations reversed. 'Of course. Tell me what's happened.'

'It's the estate; a lot of trouble here. We have a newly discovered gold mine near our boundary. The council approved permits for mining, and there are great hopes for its future potential.'

'Wow, gold. I always knew your estate was a treasure, but this is real news.'

'And it's not all as great as you'd think. There's flocking prospectors who've come and set up their own camps without permission. It's turned into a shanty camp, and it's bordering my land. Locals are up in arms and blaming me for not opposing them strongly enough. It's already impacting on our access road. Now I have village protesters outside, and a growing camp lured by dreams of riches untold.'

'I see your problem,' Hamish answered. 'All that glitters, as the saying goes.'

'We've lost bookings for the estate, and the local police tried and failed to intervene. The council have been no help, and they approved the permit for the first mining area. They just didn't expect a stampede of copycat prospectors. Ginny is about to have our first baby any time soon, and it's all making an already stressful situation much worse.'

'Have you tried speaking to the company? The police? The council?'

'Not with much success.' Hamish heard the desperation in his friend's voice. 'I was caught up with event-planning for a major conference we'd had scheduled. Only now we've lost the booking because of the mayhem putting the client off. We also had a huge wedding planned for the weekend after, and they've cancelled too with a lot of hard feelings. This is a hurtful blow for our business. We just want to sort out the problem. I could do with your wisdom. Sorry, I know it's asking a lot.'

'Of course,' Hamish said smoothly. 'We need to step up the police intervention and council support. The situation as regards mining permits needs to be clarified and acted on. And you need to make your presence felt with the police. Just because one company has the go-ahead doesn't mean gold fever can allow people to ride roughshod over the neighbourhood. You up for that?'

'Absolutely. Do your 'diplomatic, resolution-seeking lawyer with full possession of the facts' impression. Please come and give me some advice. You're welcome to stay for a while. I'd really appreciate it. And I don't say that lightly.'

'Of course I'll come, Cam,' Hamish told him. Though another thought snagged at his conscience. What about Callie? He really didn't want her staying in Bracken Cottage on her own, especially now she was being pursued by some strange bloke he didn't know from Adam. Since he'd seen the local busybody mechanics-fixing brigade, he was doubly wary. Something about Fraser set off warning bells. 'Can I ask a favour? I have company. Can I bring a friend with me?'

Cam paused for a beat. 'We have a twenty-bedroom listed building on a Highland estate. Lodge buildings for guests too, and a guest annexe big enough for a party of ten. How could I possibly not fit you in?'

Hamish knew what his friend was thinking — that he rarely dated. He was very private in affairs of the heart, so this was a first.

'Of course,' Cam said. 'I'll look forward to meeting them.'

'Yes; and before you ask aloud, her name is Callie. We've been friends since childhood. And yes I'm interested. Very interested.'

'She must be pretty special, hey? Maybe I'm not the only one with hidden gold.'

'Oh, I think she definitely is that. I hope to persuade her to come with me.'

'Then you maybe had better prepare her for some mayhem to come. This place isn't romantic in the least at present. Pop-up prospectors camping all over the place and rampaging residents out to make them think twice. I've been to quieter locales.'

'Better get there soonest, then.'

'Great. You are a lifesaver, Hamish.'

'Scrub all that. I'm a friend. And we all need to cherish and look after those.'

Hamish hung up the phone. Things must be bad to have Cam this worked up. He wondered what would face him when they got to Arrach Dean Craig Estate. It was a sixty-mile journey, but if they set off soon they'd be there in time for lunch. Now all he had to do was persuade Callie. Would she come, or resist? He'd have to find out.

Callie got in first, peeking her head around the door of the office. 'Did I just hear you mention my name?'

'Yes. But where's that bloke gone? You haven't left him alone with anything, have you? He has shifty eyes.'

'Hamish, you're as bad as he is. And he's gone. I didn't leave him unsupervised, or under any false impressions that I want him to visit again or am remotely interested in anything but his van-fixing abilities.'

'I have something to ask you, then.' Hamish grinned that she'd so ably put his worries away in a tidy pile.

'First,' she said, sending him a solemn look, 'I apologise for Fraser turning up.'

'It's okay. I'm sorry if I acted huffy. There's something about him that worries me. Turning up first thing in the morning unannounced? Following you?'

'I thought so too, but he had my phone. How else was he going to contact me, carrier pigeon?'

'I guess I'll forgive him. Did he ask you out?' Hamish couldn't believe the way that made his chest tighten as he said it out loud.

Callie blushed. 'I didn't take him up on his offers. He's not my type. Honestly.' She screwed up her nose. 'No spark. Nothing doing.'

'Don't hold back on my account.'

Callie shrugged. 'I really don't want to date him, as helpful as he's been. So what plans are you hatching? I thought we were going to do some photoshoots out in the glens?'

'We'll have to reschedule. You have a choice. I have to leave, but you could come with me. All I can tempt you with is the fact we'd be staying in one of the region's most impressive estate's luxurious surroundings. It has a waiting list for weddings like you wouldn't believe. I'm talking a historic treasure, four-poster beds, grounds fit for royalty. But they're having a bit of a crisis and need my help.'

Callie's eyes widened and she didn't say a word. Then she softly answered, 'Well it's hardly a big ask. It's not like I have much to pack. In fact I've nothing much to take with me. And it'll keep Fraser off my back.' She crossed her arms over her chest and laughed. 'Count me in. As nice as this place is, I'm not letting you upstage me in the accommodation stakes. Sounds like you have company whether you want it or not.'

Hamish grinned at her from his seat at the desk. 'When we get near to Inverness, I'll stop off for a detour so you can buy some clothes. My treat. After the ram vandalism, I feel I owe you replacements. How does that sound?'

'Sold. I'm in! I do love to shop.'

'Correct answer,' he replied softly. 'So go grab your bag, and you can help me get my photography kit in the car. Ever been a photographer's assistant before?'

'No, but I think I'm about to get a crash course.'

Hamish suddenly felt excitement swirl at their surprise imminent adventure. And it wasn't just the trip or the fun vibe. It was the woman he'd fallen for. Out of her boring routine, and with her prior prickly air cast aside, she was startling. So much for wanting a quiet break. Now there was just no stopping her.

She turned to face him. 'Sounds like

we've a plan. But you also need to get this straight in your head, Hamish. There's only one man's spark I want to pursue. It's you! You've worked hard to convince me we can work to tentatively transform things. So let's go and have an adventure together.'

8

Callie piled her splurge purchases on the counter as the assistant carefully scanned their price cards with steady beeps.

'We may have to hire an extra car now. Or at least get a trailer,' Hamish informed her, pursing his lips.

Callie searched his face but he stayed deadpan. Then when Hamish and the attendant laughed in unison, she scowled at being teased. 'They were bargains.'

'That's okay then. But isn't four nightshirts a little over-prepared for a three-night stay?' He smirked.

'The patterns were too cute to choose from. You're just being difficult.' She didn't care; she had enjoyed the pleasure of a chance to shop and buy some clothes to replace her ram-attack relics. Plus, if she was going somewhere fancy, she needed to keep standards high. She had new jeans, nightwear, a cute dress, some tops, and a lovely floaty skirt in a sheer but lined floral fabric. Plus shoes, because all she'd taken with her was trainers. All in all, she'd done well. And she didn't want to meet Hamish's friends looking like she'd been ravaged by local wildlife.

Her hunch proved right when the sight of Arrach Dean Craig Estate brought a whole new league of wonderland. Even on a drizzly change-able day, it roared of its pedigree as a rare, classy location. 'They live here? Oh my good grief! This is out of this world!' The sight of a house so beautiful that it could have come straight from a period drama made her gape. Her heart beat faster at the perfection of the location. It sat resplendent, atop a hill in the distance, graced by swaths of majestic pine trees and rolling grounds with a lime-tree-lined avenue approach. Callie wanted Hamish to stop the car so she could commit it to memory.

'You'll see it close up soon enough,'

he said when she asked. 'And you'll be able to wander in it to your heart's content. Cam and Ginny get a kick out of first-time visitors.'

'It's fabulous, even in this drizzly rain.' In the distance she spied ornate gardens, an ancient-looking botanic greenhouse, and waterfalls as the backdrop. She felt like a kid seeing a rollercoaster park for the first time and knowing she had an all-day all-areas access ticket, and grinned, engulfed in her own joy. 'I mean, talk about wow-factor. This puts TV shows to shame. Have you been here before?'

'A couple of times,' Hamish answered. 'Cam and Ginny were married here. It was quite an affair. And they were blessed with a beautiful sunny day, so you can imagine it was pretty stunning.'

'I'm jealous. I don't even like weddings, but that must've been quite a gig.'

'It was.' He grinned at her. 'I'd've loved to have you with me as my plus-one.'

'We're really staying there?' she gasped, incredulous. 'I can't wait to see inside, and inspect the grounds.'

'I'd expect nothing less of you. Cameron is old Scottish landed gentry. He also just happens to be the nicest chap you could ever meet. We met in London at a law dinner.'

'Is he a lawyer too, then?'

'No. Cameron's a gentleman farmer-cum-events and locations organiser. His estate's in high demand for film work and weddings. And sometimes he hosts conferences and big shows. Not to mention Ginny being a landscape gardener of note. She's quite famous. They host some big RHS gardening events here too.'

Callie couldn't wait to get there, but when they reached the gates she was in for a shock. They'd arrived in light rain, and a huddle of raincoat-clad people bearing large placards flanked the large gates. As soon as they saw their car, a woman in a blue mac ran up to the window and started chanting 'Stop the

167

prospector camp' right at them. A man joined her, echoing the chant.

'Sorry,' Hamish said. 'I forgot to fill you in on all this. It's part of the reason Cam called me.'

'The locals aren't happy?' Callie whispered. 'What is this prospector business?'

'A new mine was given the go-ahead after gold was discovered here, but now there's a settlement of wannabe gold-diggers on Cam's boundary land. And it's growing by the week. Cam's wife is expecting a special delivery of her own soon, too.'

'That's shocking. Can't he get the police involved?'

'He's tried, but with little impact, and now he's losing estate business.'

Callie shook her head at the grave situation. 'You think you can succeed where others have failed? No offence, but there's only one of you, and I don't think you've packed your superhero costume.'

Hamish raised his eyebrows. 'When a

friend's in need, I'll give it my best shot. I'm not saying I'll succeed, but I'll certainly try, and I do have connections.' He gave her a grim look that told her he meant his words.

And that was what she adored about him. He really was an old-fashioned man of honour who'd stick his neck out for a friend or any cause he truly believed in. Callie itched to hug him and admit to her weakness, but doubts and reservations still crowded in her mind.

Instead, she let her hand slip to touch his briefly on the gear stick. 'I'd feel brave having you in my corner,' she whispered. 'Always knew you were hero material.'

Their gazes met and held. 'Count on it, Callie. I'm here whenever you need me. Always.'

Her breaths came fast and her heart rate had tripled in speed. Just from that hot look, from the amazing man in the seat next to her. She blew out a little breath. 'Looks like you'll have your work cut out for you. I don't envy your task. You really think you can influence these warring parties?'

'Cam's at his wits' end. Looks like I may have drawn the short straw on this dispute.'

'I think it's commendable that you're prepared to try,' Callie said just as Hamish got out of the car and walked to the entry phone system. She observed that he exchanged some words with the group but kept focused on his task of getting inside the estate. Then he got back into the car to wait for the gates to part. With serendipity, the gates opened and the grumpy gathered throng moved aside as he drove into the estate.

Once they got fully into the grounds and the gates had closed behind them, Callie asked, 'If you don't mind me asking, how can there be prospectors in here with such high security?'

'Your guess is as good as mine. I think it's boundary land. I figure we'll soon find out.'

'It's such a shame to mar such an

extraordinary place.'

'Ruins the romance?' said Hamish. 'Of course, I can be persuaded to summon some if you feel inclined.'

Callie pushed his arm. 'You don't need encouragement, do you?'

He grinned, but she figured he was masking his real anxieties about the situation ahead. She saw the giveaway flex of his jaw. Was her legal-supremo negotiations ambassador biting off more than he could chew here? Callie worried that, as good as his motives were, he just might be.

★ ★ ★

'When Cam told me Hamish was bringing a female companion, I almost fell over!' Ginny exclaimed before they'd even got hellos out of the way. Ginny Henderson had a mass of copper spiral curls, a sparklingly vibrant manner, and the biggest baby bump in the north of Scotland. Surely it had to be triplets in there.

Callie stared in shock. 'Please say you didn't. Fall over, I mean.'

'No. If I had, I'd probably bounce. Cushioned for a soft landing,' Ginny laughed, brushing off the concern. 'I can't wait to have this baby.'

Not triplets then, Callie found herself confirming in her head. She smiled to cover her confusion.

'I just want to be free of the too-big-for-everything tummy. Shouldn't complain, but I can't help it. I can't even weed the garden, and I'm consigned to greenhouse seed-sowing only. How unfair! It's against my every inclination.'

Callie hardly knew Ginny, but she already realised she liked her. Especially when she grabbed her arm and led her into a house that vied with any large historic stately abode she'd had the privilege of visiting at cost.

'Wow!' Callie exclaimed.

'Don't go all over-awed on me. Everybody does. It gets boring when they go into raptures over this place and avoid me. Seriously, I'll take you on the proper tour later; or Archie, one of our guides, is the best in our gang, and he'll take you round with full gusto. So tell me all — how did you meet?'

This woman really didn't hang about before interrogation. Callie prised her attention from a wall full of austere paintings and menacing stag's-head trophies as Ginny pulled her away.

Cam called out from behind them, 'Woah there, Gin. I know you've been a bit deprived of female company since your sister absconded, volunteering for a job in the rainforest, but put Callie down for five minutes. Let her breathe. Can't the girl even have a cup of tea first?'

Cam Henderson was a very tall man who wore country casuals and sported long mid-length floppy dark blond hair and a puppy-like disposition. He owned a beguiling schoolboy smile that belied his years. And he was clearly in love with his crazy wife. 'Let's not forget our manners, Pookie Toes.'

Callie's gaze flicked to Hamish, and

his flat glance told her this was nothing out of the norm for this pair. Then Hamish burst out laughing, and Callie wondered for a moment if he was being rude. She chastised him with a reprimanding stare.

'You two still persist with that crazy pet names thing?' He looked at Callie and saw her expression. 'It's a running joke. They started it as a bet. The person who gets the most points for outrageous pet-names in company gets a forfeit. What can it be this time? I imagine champagne is out, given the pregnancy.'

'Chocolate truffles usually.' Ginny rubbed her tummy and screwed up her nose. 'Stop spoiling the fun. I want him to move my acers in the oriental garden, and the loser gets the job. I can hardly do it in this condition, can I?'

'You're not going to call each other mad names the whole time we're here?' Hamish persisted, smiling and shaking his head.

'We'll stop if you two take over, or let

us in on your romance secrets.' Ginny rubbed her hands in glee. 'I want to know it all. How long have you been dating? How did he ask you out? Where was the first kiss? All of it. Full, uncensored, comprehensive Technicolor.'

'Is she still as bad as you remember, Hamish?' Cam asked.

Hamish, now red along the cheek-bones, rubbed his jaw. 'Much, much worse. Can't you keep that woman of yours under control, Cam?'

'I could try,' he confided, shaking his head like a life-weary stalwart. 'But I really don't fancy my chances of winning. Ever.'

★　★　★

They had tea in an enormous natural wood kitchen-cum-lounge at the back of the estate overlooking the oriental garden Ginny had mentioned. Callie could imagine no more heavenly place on earth, and savoured every detail and each special moment.

And boy, what an oriental garden! It

showcased a gleaming black lacquer pagoda and a quaint scarlet bridge over a burbling stream. Callie hoped that as soon as the drizzle stopped they might venture out, like stepping into a beautiful impressionist painting that begged to be explored.

'Is this where you live day to day?' Callie asked, sipping her tea.

'Yes,' Ginny answered. 'The main rooms are for visitors and special events. We live in this back annexe. Best part is it's got my favourite area of the garden. Though the big fountain out front always gets the most press.'

This part of the building was more contemporary modern architect's creation than period fine dining, but the setting was still breathtaking. What the situation lacked in the pomp and grandeur Callie expected of such a house, the tea more than made up for. It was high tea with cakes, sandwiches, scones and lashings of steaming welcome tea in mugs. It made her feel immediately part of the gang. 'This is gorgeous,' she said.

'And Callie knows her stuff, so that's praise indeed,' Hamish interjected, 'because she runs a tea shop. Well, a coffee shop/bakery, but high teas are her big speciality.'

'So how do we rate?' Ginny teased. 'Fair to middling, or full points?'

'I've been to the Chelsea Flower Show, so I know how exacting you garden people can be,' Callie said. 'I'm giving a gold medal for best in show. Definitely not a silver gilt for this effort.' Proving her words, she demolished the end of her mini-choux pastry with relish.

Ginny grinned, pleased with the compliment, and Hamish winked at her. 'You see,' she explained, 'people come here and they assume we eat off Wedgwood and drink out of champagne flutes in the main dining room at every meal. It's all for show, for the guided tours and the tourists. Most of the time I'm an ordinary lass who lives in my garden in my wellies with a tin mug and a flask, when I'm not indisposed with a big kicking baby bump, that is; or we live in the back of the house in these private apartments, eating egg and chips and watching Netflix like everybody else.'

'I guess we all just fall for the dream,' Callie said. 'You mean Cam doesn't dress up like Mr. Darcy? I'm so disappointed.'

'If you fancy, after dinner tonight we'll all have a wander into the main drawing room and library for fun,' Ginny offered. 'Will that keep you happy?'

'Don't go to any trouble for me.'

'I want to. I sense you're a bit in love with it all.'

'Well then, that would be amazing, Ginny.'

'Of course I can't guarantee that I can get Cam or Hamish to dress up in a frock coat or full Highland kilt attire to make it historically accurate. It'll just be the blokes in their jeans most likely.'

'And here was me imagining I'd be

dressing up for dinner tonight with butler service,' Callie said with a giggle. 'I'd brought my Marie Antoinette dress specially.'

'Hope you brought the wig too,' Ginny said, then laughed heartily. 'I like you, Callie. Hamish has found a star. We're going to get on a treat. We share the same sense of humour, which is a relief; Cam doesn't have any sense of humour at all. It's most annoying. Coo-kaboo Cammie isn't as much fun for me as he should be. But I think he's more in a tizzy about the baby than me.'

But it isn't just the baby's arrival he has on his mind, is it? thought Callie. He had gold-grabbers and protesters; revenue lost and problems unsolved. Quite a lot of trouble on his doorstep, but Callie didn't want to highlight it.

Hamish pulled a face at the mention of the nickname. 'Coo-kaboo? Seriously? Now that's a hideous imprint I won't ever erase from my brain. I may even have nightmares now.'

'Don't be mean, Hamish,' Callie laughed.

179

'Now I'll have to think up something awful for you. It'll have to be something of a showstopper.'

Ginny interjected, 'Like Honey-Bunny Hamish?'

'That'll do nicely,' Callie said, winking at Cam. 'I'm already getting the feeling that Cam's quite long-suffering, and just as crazy as his exuberant wife. How else does he put up with the nicknames?'

Cam stood. 'Let me take you both to your rooms so you can get settled. I need to talk to Hamish about the issues on the estate. Do you mind very much, Callie, if Ginny takes you for a tour of the garden while we're busy, now that the drizzle's stopped? Though you may still need a jacket in case it starts again. I won't keep your man long.'

'Of course. I'd love to see the grounds.'

Ginny grinned. 'Did you bring wellingtons? Don't worry; I have a boot-room full of pairs. We'll go seek some out.'

'Sounds like a plan,' said Cam.

'Not a problem; I'm keen to get

180

down to things and formulate a strategy soonest,' Hamish told him. 'Enjoy the tour, ladies. And maybe when you get back you can show me the highlights for some photography. That a deal, Callie?' He winked at her in a way that made her know 'photography' was a code word for solo time. And she quite liked that he'd done that. She wanted time one-to-one with him.

'I'll keep vigilant and hope the rain passes,' she said. 'Can I take your spare camera with me?' She surprised herself with the question, which had only popped into her head just then. But she itched to record these images for trip souvenirs.

'Of course. I'll fetch it,' Hamish told her. 'Didn't realise you liked to take photos yourself.'

'I couldn't possibly come as a private guest to a place this amazing and not record every moment to relive again,' she told him, and she saw the joy sparkling in his eyes when he looked at her.

'Are you scared that Callie might upstage you with better shots?' Ginny asked. 'We know how competitive Hamish gets. I'll make sure I take you to the best places — my own private special corners for contemplation.'

'I'll take holiday snaps, but they'll still be special to me,' Callie answered. 'And I'll duly report back later for critique. I'll try my best,' she added, her insides smiling like a sunburst. 'See you later, Honey-Bunny.'

The shocked stare he gave her was priceless.

9

Ginny and Callie went outside to wander in the delightful surroundings of a recently rain-doused garden, now bathed in bright sun. It really did smell divine; fresh and inviting. The birdsong above them only added to the pull.

Callie inhaled a lungful of Highland foliage with bells on and was almost tempted to do a *Sound of Music* arms-out twirl. 'I love it here!' she said to Ginny, who laughed in a half-snort-half-giggle. 'You're so lucky. You do realise you live in a real life fairy-tale, don't you? You probably even have fairies and pixies who live out here.'

'No, just a grumpy old troll. You already met my husband.'

Callie tutted. 'Now stop pretending, and own up to the fact you're crazy about each other.' She knew the slight was fake and that Ginny and Cam were as in love as any couple could ever be.

'I do love him, really. And yes, I feel the magic too when I'm out here gardening. Though lately not so much. I've been like a grumpy she-bear with a sore paw. It's all got a little too much to handle.'

'How come?'

'The gold prospectors who are converging here without permission. The ones Cam's brought Hamish to help us find a resolution with. Not only have they interfered with our business, but they've also made a mess and upended things with our neighbours. The locals blame us, as they border our land, but we're as keen for them to go as they are. We're caught in the middle by virtue of our location.'

'But why are the locals lobbying you so hard? Why not the council or authorities?'

'Local feeling is we've let the problem persist for too long. In reality, Cam and I have been tied up with hospital appointments. I had some high liver readings taken at antenatal checks and so have had to go in regularly to be monitored — nothing bad, just precautionary. And it distracted us; we figured the baby came first.'

Callie felt deeply sorry for Ginny's plight. 'Nobody could ever blame you for that.'

'Unfortunately, the villagers don't understand all the variables. The protester settlement camp is sizeable. We've tried all approaches, from tippy-toe gentle to 'come on time to call the cops with sirens'. Nothing's worked.'

'You think Hamish will have more success?'

Ginny sighed deeply and shoved her hands deep into her wax-jacket pockets. 'He's the one person I'd trust to sort out any legal crisis, so yes. We're losing money every day they're here. Word gets round fast in these parts, and it's not exactly in keeping with the high-class clientele we strive to attract.'

'And have the police come? Why can't they do more?'

'They didn't have enough officers to make any impact. I think the local force is too small to cope. We haven't persuaded the force back yet, nor have we been able to persuade the residents to stop the protests outside.'

'And that's where Hamish comes in. Persuasive, facts-at-fingertips lawyer.'

'Exactly. I'd rather not have all this aggro going on when my baby comes home. I'd prefer to have lovely memories of bringing the future estate heir or heiress here without placards being brandished.'

'You're having a tough old time,' Callie told her.

Ginny, clearly uncomfortable and needing to move, rose and stretched. She pulled a beautiful peach-coloured rose for Callie to smell. The fragrance of a floral cocktail burst for her senses. And then Ginny sat again in a fresh position, absently patting her bump. 'I've been caged up in the house because of the baby. Cam's been worried about the liver problem because it's his first baby, and he's stalking me in case of any problems. He's watching me like a hawk for fear I dare to lift something as heavy as a baby catalogue. He won't even let me make a cup of tea half the time. And don't get me started on his mother. We've had to send her away. She was threatening to go down to the paddock and remove the gold prospectors herself. Imagine!'

'It's only because they care. And nobody likes to feel like everything's out of their control.'

Ginny smiled. 'I'm an outdoors girl; and as delighted and excited as I am to have the baby, I'm thinking the sooner I get the bambino outdoors beside me in its pram, gurgling as I prune and dig, the happier I'll be. If Hamish can just sort out one of the conflict problems, that'll be a huge relief.'

Callie felt the sadness in Ginny and rubbed her new friend's arm. 'Enjoy your pregnancy. It's a precious time, and should be perfect and special.' She took no harm from the fact that Ginny couldn't ever suspect the darkness in her heart because of her own fertility woes. But then the woman would be appalled if she knew she'd trampled painful emotional terrain.

Callie cleared her throat and forced a bright smile. 'Though I can see why you love it here. It's fabulous. Imagine playing hide-and-seek in this garden. Possibly the best location ever.'

'And talking of fab, this new thing with you and Hamish . . . He's never brought a date with him before. Ever. Which tells me he's crazy about you.'

'He's not dating me. We're friends. Good friends. We go way back.'

'I believe you. Thousands would see the flush on your cheeks when you avoid eyeballing me and disbelieve every word you say. You may not be dating, but I think you both want it. What's holding you back?'

'You think I fancy Hamish, and he fancies me?' Callie did 'as if' eyes at her. Wasn't it easier to deflect, just as Ginny did about her husband? 'I'm not sure we can convert what we share as friends to romance, Ginny.'

Ginny took her hand and held it firmly. 'I want full disclosure details. How it started; how long it's been going on. How great he is at kissing. Come on, give a very large pregnant lady some thrills. You do realise he's totally got his heart on his sleeve when you're around, and can't take his eyes off you. I can read 'lovesick' on him like a neon sign. Impart your juicy info and admit what's been happening.'

Callie sensed she'd have no peace unless she agreed. 'No dating. No kissing. We're childhood pals. He used to help me make ice-lollies in the summer and rescue his sister and me when we got stuck up trees or found a wasps' nest and screamed like banshees. Linley and I have been best friends since forever. Hamish is her big, brave brother. We're getting to know each other over again and seeing where that leads.' She kept the fact she was lying about the kissing a closely guarded secret. And they really weren't an official item yet. Possibly ever.

'I see,' Ginny scoffed. 'Do you want me to use security cameras to capture his glances at you later? It's incriminating evidence. He looks like he worships and adores you.'

Callie felt her heart speed inside her ribcage. Was it true? Was Hamish really keen on her? Or was it, as she suspected, that Ginny's high hormones had her seeing romantic mirages without substance? 'Whatever you say. We'll be married in the spring with dancing cherubs cavorting through the church. Or pigs will fly, one or the other.'

'Callie, I don't say this lightly, but give him the chance he craves. You couldn't ask for a better bloke to fall for.'

'but I'm just a humble baker, and Hamish is a legend in his own legal lunchbreak. I'm just a girl who runs a café, bakes passably, and doesn't even know what she wants to do with her life anymore.'

'They call those things epiphanies. Sounds like you're having one.'

'And it sounds like you've been watching too many chick flicks in your last trimester.' Callie grimaced.

'I can see what he sees in you. You don't take yourself seriously, and that's just his type.'

'Next you'll be telling me you see divine signs in my too-loud laugh and that I have one foot slightly bigger than the other. I saw you noticed that in the boot-room with the wellingtons, but you were much too polite to say, and for that I'm grateful.' When things got too personal or close to the bone, Callie had always deflected with self-deprecation. Usually it worked, and this time was no exception, with Ginny hooting with laughter.

'It must cause you untold issues when you shop for stilettos.'

Callie pointed her boot-clad foot to emphasise her point. 'Fortunately I never wear them. I'm a flats girl all the way. Flat shoes, flat chest. I know my limits. And Hamish is one of them. We're friends, not flirt partners. So put a sock in it and let's talk about plants. I want to pick your brains. Come on, let's go and explore your grounds before more rain falls. I want you to show me your rarest specimens, please.'

★ ★ ★

A half-hour meeting with the local police force's regional chief inspector saw more promises for prompt action than had hitherto been witnessed in weeks. He'd even admitted that their staffing situation wasn't ideal, and promised more manpower and a fresh offensive to take charge. Of course it helped that Hamish had a friend who knew someone senior who knew somebody else who could pull strings.

'Do you think we're going to get somewhere?' Hamish asked. It was a rhetorical question, because he was pretty pleased with what he'd been promised: action, the following day if promised: action, the following day if not sooner. The settlement would be visited and encouraged to vacate; they had no official permits. They'd be escorted off site within the week.

Hamish was thankful that he also had high-up connections in other forces, lending him expertise and support staff. No organisation, even a police force, likes others muscling in on their turf and underlining their inadequacies. It frustrated Hamish that things like networking always boosted priorities; but as long as it worked, he would be satisfied for now. Cam needed calm before the baby, and business and order resuming again soon were the best outcomes possible.

Cam shook his hand and let out a loud sigh of relief. 'They've promised a police presence by tomorrow. Thanks, Hamish. I couldn't have achieved this without you.'

'Let's hope they're better than the last lot you had,' Hamish remarked. 'And don't get too carried away; they haven't left yet. The situation still needs careful handling. The police will also have a quiet word with the key activists from the village.'

'I'm feeling better already. You inspire confidence.'

'Good. But we won't celebrate yet. Action speaks louder than words. I'll take a keen interest in tomorrow's events. And later tomorrow I have a meeting with the chief reporter for your local paper — it seems the lad needs a good grounding in the rules of objective journalism. His village-rousing articles haven't helped encourage calm, and I'm not sure they had the sensationalised substance he claimed. I intend to make him see that he might have some culpability in the matter.'

'What can I say, Hamish? What would I do without you? I really owe you.'

'I'm sure Ginny would keep you occupied without me.' Hamish grinned. 'She's some woman.'

'She's nice too,' Cam told Hamish

after they'd left the police station in Blandinny.

'Who? That WPC on the desk? You're married and shouldn't notice.'

'No. Your plus one, Callie. Ginny's taken a real shine to her. She says you've met 'the one'.'

Hamish swatted his comment away like an unruly insect out for sport, trying to play it cool yet knowing by the way his skin felt that his ears had gone beet red and he'd given himself away. This was so not cool. He kept his head much better when he performed in court. Thank goodness he wasn't this easy when in professional mode. How come affairs of the heart — most specifically Callie issues — had him acting like a lovesick schoolboy?

'You suit each other very well. Ginny thinks she's the best thing since an extending garden hoe. That's a compliment, by the way. She says I'm better than a well-forked compost heap, if that helps with perspective.'

'High praise indeed,' said Hamish, laughing as they walked back to his car. 'I'll tell Callie about the hoe thing. Better than garden tools. The sky's the limit.'

Cam shrugged. 'You know what I mean. Ginny has a nose for the good lads. Or great lasses even. Callie's a keeper. Question is, do you think so too? You can't bring her here and then expect Ginny to let you ever go after anybody else. She'll be calling you on a weekly basis to make sure you're engaged within months. Expect an invitation to bring her back here when the baby's arrived. And be prepared for some interrogation about when you're going to get really serious. I see Ginny meddling in this nonstop. You've been warned.'

Perhaps bringing Callie Dewar here wasn't his greatest brainwave, Hamish thought. He'd brought her slap-bang into his private inner circle. Introduced her to his dearest friends. Done for her what he'd never done with any other woman. Partly because he knew Callie would be loved and accepted by them. Because Callie was Callie — the kind of woman you could bank on.

Hamish raised his eyebrows and tried to concentrate on walking back to the car without tripping over his feet or his words. What was he waking up to here? That Callie was his pinnacle? That she mattered enough for him to bend rules? That he did want her in his future picture? For good? Was he testing himself in this? The thought scared him so much he stumbled, and Cam reached out to grab his arm in case he walked right into a nearby parked car. Talk about a wake-up call. Callie mattered. Callie already was in his inner sanctum. And if he had his way, he'd do everything he could to make her stay there. It felt like a blinding flash of conviction.

So a confession was the best way to go here. 'She won't have me, Cam. Believe me, I've tried for a long time. I've tried everything — flirting, attentive friendship, harmless funny fellow, flirting with other women even. None of it makes a dent. She always knocks me back. Now my aunt and sister have intervened to get us stuck in a lodge together, double-booked. And while I've seen a glimmer that she might like me underneath it all, there's still something holding her back. I see her resist; I can read it in her face when it happens. It's like there's a wall I can't get past. And I don't know what else to do.'

'Maybe she's pining for somebody else. Or is it something from her past?'

'I thought that — the past thing. We once kissed and I got things really wrong. For ages I think she held that against me. I'd hurt her. But I see that it's more than that. There's something Callie can't trust anybody with, especially not me. And she's single as far as I know.'

'What's that about, then?'

Cam unlocked the car and they both got inside. 'Damned if I know.

But I'm back here hoping that if I keep at it long and hard enough and wear her down, she might wake up and realise I'm not so bad really. I'd thought I was a pretty good catch, until Callie refused me for so long that I started to think I have a body hygiene problem nobody's dared to tell me about.'

Cam slapped him on the back as he turned the key in the ignition and prepped to move off. 'You have it bad for her, I see it. And it's not you. You're fine, in both looks and odour. There must be a reason she's staying coy. Ever asked her outright? Sat her down and told her what you think? Opened your heart up? Then maybe she'd do the same.'

Hamish stared at his friend, and only then realised he hadn't — not outright. Not properly. He'd guessed there was something up lately. She'd said it was café woes, but even then he'd never actually sat her down and asked for answers. Maybe like with the gold rush problem, he should try to expose the truth.

'I'll do that, Cam. You're right. Have it out. Why didn't I think of that? Am I really that dense and rubbish?'

'You may have an insightful legal brain, but you've no sense when it comes to women. Not like me. I'm a Jedi master. Watch and learn.'

'Unlike you, TootsieScoots. Pardon me if I don't genuflect in your presence, oh hallowed Lady Whisperer.'

Cam grinned. 'Talk to her. Ask her outright. Best course of action. Call yourself a fancy, clever lawyer, and I've just had to identify the loophole to you?'

Hamish breathed deeply, then added, 'Well, we can't all be this handsome and gifted without some tiny flaws creeping in.'

'Whatever you say, Hamish.' Cam grinned widely, then started back for the estate. 'Just don't go getting that printed as your business card quite yet. And maybe think about working harder on impressing that lass. That's one area you don't want to make mistakes in. I sense winning Callie is your biggest-ever priority.'

10

'You sure you don't mind that we aren't eating in the big dining room?' Ginny asked. 'I forgot that tomorrow we have a tour booked that hasn't cancelled on us — a group of church ladies who are getting a full tour. I'd hate for them to put in a complaint about the tapestries smelling of our spicy food.'

Callie shook her head. 'I don't mind at all. And if this means I get that Thai curry I ordered, I'm all for it.'

Two men brought in tureens with warmers for their 'takeaway' feast done country-house style. A fast-food delivery at Arrach Dean Craig meant a caterer with a van and an array of treats over street food.

'We don't often get food delivered in,' Ginny confided. 'And I'm clamouring for Chinese.'

'I believe Hamish is a big fan of

crispy duck, so he'll be right with you.'

'Then he's in luck. It's on the menu.'

The vast stripped-pine table in their annexe was covered in plates and trays. It felt more like being at a wedding with a buffet table over a night at home having a ready-meal.

'We don't get out much,' said Ginny. 'And Rosa is our regular caterer here. I can't compete with her amazing culinary skills so I'm not about to try. Also I didn't know what you both liked, so I've gone for a selection. Hopefully you'll find something appetising. So, tuck in! They say a hot curry can bring babies on, and I haven't had spicy food in ages. Will a Chinese curry count?'

'No idea. All I know is that this is delicious, and if your baby knows a good thing, it won't spoil this feast by deciding to arrive tonight. I'm blown away; it's so tasty!'

Hamish spooned chicken curry and duck pancakes onto his plate and waggled his eyebrows at Callie. 'Talking about me again?'

Callie laughed. 'I said the food was tasty, not you.'

'Can't blame a chap for trying.'

Cam nodded to the food and urged, 'Fill your boots, Callie. But pace yourself. Rosa also does fab desserts.'

Callie intended to savour it all as she scooped more jasmine rice onto her plate. And from the very first mouthful she was in Oriental heaven. Food and garden views both.

'Don't eat too much, mind,' Ginny reminded her. 'You haven't seen our pop-up sweet trolley yet! Or the chocolate fondue that's going to leave you whimpering for more!'

★   ★   ★

'You look lovely,' Hamish whispered beside Callie's ear as she stood on the terrace at dusk, watching the bats swoop for flies as their late-night repast. The 'private tour' of the formal rooms had really made Callie's stay complete. She was still marvelling over it.

'Thank you. Nice of you to notice.' She felt the light breeze whip her hair into her face and pushed it away.

'Oh, I've noticed all right. The food was incredible. But it's you who's a feast for the eyes. I mean that. I really do.'

Full of amazing lip-smacking food and fine wine, Callie wondered if she'd actually get much wear out of the new clothes she'd bought. She was beginning to think she might just pop buttons tonight. She'd eaten too much, but with such a spread and great company it was hard not to get lost in the moment. She'd honestly had one of the best nights of her life. And tonight she felt like a whole new person. She was wearing the floaty skirt from Inverness paired with a gypsy ivory gauzy top.

'Now you're just flattering me. What are you after?'

'You know me. I just want to spend time with my favourite lass.'

She felt her cheeks heat as he stood

beside her and his warm arm crept around her shoulders. She loved the feel of his height and latent strength beside her in such close proximity.

'Aren't you cold, Cal? I can fetch you a blanket if you want.'

'I'm fine.' She turned her head to watch Ginny and Cam. They were snuggling on a love-seat by the doors to the terrace, huddled in a plaid rug and looking very much in love. Ginny caught her watching and gave her a mighty thumbs-up.

Callie whispered, 'Your friends have rose-tinted intentions. They're united on selling you as my next Prince Charming. Little do they realise I've known you way too long to fall for the solve-it-all smooth-lawyer lines.'

'I haven't solved things yet. And the only thing I want to get onto are the hard-to-crack barriers that still stand between us. Why do you keep pushing me away, Callie? Haven't I proved my sincerity?'

'Hamish, you're a wonderful chap.

But a love affair with me really might not be the fun ride you imagine it to be. You're always confident, in charge, in control. You have such potential that it scares me. I honestly can't compete.'

'Compete? Callie, I love you. But this isn't a contest. I suspect you're hiding something important from me, and all I can say is, whatever that secret is, I have your back one hundred percent. And I'll do everything in my power to bring you peace.'

Callie turned to face him. His grey eyes challenged her in the light from the house. A man could never understand her struggle, no matter how well-intentioned he was. She felt less of a woman; less whole somehow, yet a victim of her own body's reality. She was a female failure with a blighted outlook no romance could soften.

'You make me sound heartless,' she said. 'I'm trying to warn you off gently and you won't take my hints.'

'Because I think you're amazing, but I never know where I stand. And for the record, my friends haven't stopped going on about how wonderful you are since I brought you here. I'm talking full-on sales-pitch and an offer of a wedding venue for free when we're ready.'

Callie gasped, then looked around her, taking in the full experience and committing it to memory, and adding her regrets to an impossible event. 'It is a pretty great place for a wedding. Best I've ever seen. Unfortunately I don't think I'm right for the role.'

'Does that mean you refuse to consider me?'

'Hamish, you don't want to marry me. You're just at a crossroads and confused.'

'You're evading what I asked you — I want to know where I stand. Not on weddings or big future declarations; just in terms of enough hope that maybe you could consider me as a bloke you'd actually like to date. You did let it slip you loved me, remember. Even though you changed it to 'like' with your next breath.'

It figured he'd catch and remember her slip. 'Damn. Can't I take that back? Maybe I had a fever.' She pushed her hand across her forehead. 'Yes, my forehead is warm. A definite fever.'

'No, you can't renege. Your words have kept the smile on my face since I heard them. It's all I can think about, and I'm only resisting punching the air in joy by the tiniest thread.'

Then she remembered his desire for children; the family he and the rest of the Gordons expected. A weight pushed against her chest and her lungs laboured. The diagnosis she didn't want to face reared, sweeping all his fun, joy and romance away like a huge doom-laden broom. 'Maybe you deserve better than me, that's all. You deserve more than I can offer.'

'Trust me to be the judge of that one,' he said. 'I'm a grown-up.'

'And maybe I'm not the kind of future material you think I am. I'm not into long-term future planning. Or families. I don't plan on having children, for one thing. You've already mentioned wanting kids. Could you really see yourself without them in your future, Hamish?'

His chest raised as he inhaled a long breath. Then he looked her straight in the eye. 'I don't care, Callie. It's you I want, not the trappings. And what's wrong with trying us out for size and just seeing how it goes? You could have the best time of your life.'

Or I could die a little each day knowing you settled for less. 'Your plan sounds crazy, mad and dangerous.'

'Trust me,' he said softly near to her ear. 'It won't be. Not if I can help it.' He took the glass from between her fingers that was nearly empty and laid it down on the flagstones out of harm's reach. Then he tugged her close. 'Just kiss me, Callie. And stop evading, worrying, and hiding behind every excuse against us you can think of. For once, just simply go with the flow and give yourself permission to follow your heart.'

He covered her mouth with his

warm, pliant, seeking lips, conveying the deep emotions he'd told her of yet she'd ducked from. But how could she deny this? He was real, all-man, and telling her ably that the fire that sparked and crackled between them had a life of its own.

'You're all that I hope for.' He held her in strong arms and kissed her again, but this time more softly, with tenderness and attentive persuasion. His best friends were watching, and most likely they'd incited him to do this, but she found she didn't care.

'Say you'll think about it?' he said. 'Say I at least stand a chance, Cal. That's all I want — some hope. We could be so great together. Your kiss tells me you feel it too.'

'I do.' And she willingly kissed him back, daring to hope and open herself a smidgeon to believe for a second that he could just have a point and be right.

'Oh Callie, you've no idea how long I've dreamed of this,' he whispered.

She knew she'd capitulated, and

given him a positive answer with her kiss, but didn't regret a nip or lick. How could going with the moment be wrong when it felt this good?

★　★　★

Hamish arrived at the tiny office of the Inverbuie *Chronicle* the next morning before eleven. He had no idea what Archie McConnell would look like, but he didn't expect him to be barely out of school, wearing trendy oversized spectacles and a shirt that was two sizes too big for him. Life was nothing if not surprising lately.

'Archie McConnell?' Hamish said. 'I'm a representative of the Henderson family from Arrach Dean Craig, and I'd like to speak to you about publishing an article.'

'That's me.' The young man drew himself up, though it barely made a difference, since he was short as well as young in terms of years. 'How can I help? Unless it's some amazing celebrity scoop, it'll have to wait til next week as we're on a deadline.'

'Truth over titillation this time, and I suggest it's high time you listened fully to all the facts and published something that reflects all sides,' said Hamish, pulling out a seat and sitting on it even though he hadn't been offered a chair.

Given the lad was the only person in the office, it was hardly major deduction work to ascertain that he was something of a one-man-band.

'Sorry — I'm just on my way out, actually,' Archie protested, and he rose from his seat.

Hamish leaned over and swiped Archie's mobile phone, hoping to stall him. 'It'll wait.' He used the tone he did when summing up in court. Concise. Clipped. Brass-tacks business-like. 'I don't think we need to shilly-shally with long backstories to this debacle. The villagers have given you all your leads.' He reached into his pocket and took out the number for the police chief he'd spoken to. 'I have authority for you to speak to the regional chief of police for quotes about how hard the Hendersons have worked to secure a resolution. I think you can hold the front page for that, don't you?'

Archie sat back down and Hamish smiled inwardly. Now he had his attention. 'Shall we begin? In short, I'm a friend of Cam Henderson's, and news coverage of the recent issues has been openly biased. You owe them coverage of their side of things. And I don't mean sound bites. I mean proper reasoned clarification.' Hamish took in the untidy paper-strewn office, the lack of staff, and the askew plaque above his desk that read 'Reporter of the Year 2015'. He wondered how the lad got that, given the shoddy skewed items he'd published. Or was he getting too cynical in his old age? He'd read the stories, all of which had been slanted to an extreme degree.

'Old news I'm afraid, unless you could get me up to the big house to get their side of things ASAP. We're going to press, but if you could get me in there today I might just be able to run something small on the front page. I'd want a full-colour photo of them, and the chance to ask my own questions.'

Hamish shook his head, then returned the reporter's phone as he handed over his own, which featured some photographs of his friends taken that morning. 'I'll happily let you use these without credit. I've saved you the job.' He had taken on esteemed, revered judges in his time and switched the norms. There was no way some fresh-in-the-post reporter with a super-sized ego was going to play swings and roundabouts on his watch and win.

'You misunderstand me, Mr. McConnell,' Hamish continued. 'I'm not here to offer anything. I'm a friend and their legal representative, and as such I'm here to tell you my clients have a genuine call to take your newspaper to court for the allegations that have been made against them recently. As a senior lawyer at the European Court of

Human Rights, I know lots of ways we can make this a lengthy, slow, painful process. I'm pretty sure your cash-strapped company CEO would far rather you dealt with this affair the easy way — with your by-line and a firm commitment to objective journalism that presents all sides fairly. That sounds like the sensible option to me.' He forced a serene smile.

'Listen, I don't have time to talk about this.' Archie stood again, but Hamish saw his upper eye tremble discernibly.

'Sit down. Because you're going to take notes, deadline or no deadline. And by the time we've finished having our chat, you're going to run a story that better reflects the truth of what's been happening and the victimisation that the Hendersons have suffered. Prominent — I'd say a new front-page headline. Because if you don't want to go to court and see me there ramping up the bills, you'd better get your fingers on the keyboard.'

Hamish watched as Archie gulped and straightened his tie. Then he pushed his specs up on the bridge of his nose. 'You often blag your way into things this way?' the reporter muttered.

Hamish stifled a grin. 'No. But I'm improvising for a friend. A friend who deserves due credit.'

'Must be a good friend,' said Archie.

'Oh he is. And he's a local business, an employer in this locale, and right now the villager actions and the media's handling of this affair are impacting on his business's viability by the day. You wouldn't want its failure and the resulting job losses to weigh on your conscience, now, would you? Much as I appreciate you're not that long in this job, you want to build a career and earn trust, surely? I can see you're a man of good sense and ethics, after all.'

Archie finally found his voice and tried to use it. Shame it emerged as more of squeak than a roar, but Hamish gave him full points for pluck. 'You can't just walk in here and start telling me what to do like this.'

'Oh, I think I can. You said that the Hendersons let the prospectors set up camp nearby. You made no attempt to speak to them to get their view.'

'They were busy each time I called.'

'With important antenatal appointments. Mrs. Henderson is expecting her first child. You chose to focus instead on protesters in all your coverage. Am I right in asserting that the key activist protesters supported the new estate access road and bridge that the Hendersons lobbied against recently? Could this be a gripe taken a step further? Might that not be a story worth exploring?'

'I don't know what you're talking about,' the reporter replied, but Hamish was gratified to note that he slowly sat down and pulled his keyboard towards him.

Hamish got out his carefully worded statement and passed it over the desk. 'This press release says it all. We'd like it to appear word for word — 'Estate Victims Caught in Middle of Protester

Prospector Stand-off. Henderson Family Find Resolution.' Shall we start, then?' Hamish waited to see just how fast the Reporter of the Year could type when a front page counted most.

★　★　★

'Callie!' The sound was unmistakable. There was an edge to the cry that had Callie at Ginny's side in seconds. She'd gone to the other room to check on the logs situation for the burners, as Callie had offered to fetch supplies. But Ginny hadn't made it to the other room before crying out and leaning against the wall for support.

'You okay?'

'Um, yes and no.'

'Contractions started?'

'I think the baby is telling me it's time . . . oh . . . nobody told me it would feel like this.' Ginny's face contorted. 'Wow, talk about nought to ninety in three seconds flat. I think he'll be a rally driver when he's older.'

'Shall I ring the midwife? Where's the number?'

'Cam's down at the settlement site; he wanted to witness the evacuation so that he wasn't being a faceless landowner. The contacts book could be on his desk.'

'Don't worry about Cam; I'll get him next. Let's get the midwife first.'

Callie flicked through the book that she eventually found on the dresser, realising as she tried to read the number with a finger under each digit that she was shaking hard. She stopped herself. *Think, focus. Act like you're in the café and you're taking charge of a bodged order — not taking charge of a baby about to be born!* Mind you, a baby about to make its first appearance in the world was way more stressful than a couple of boxes of bungled buns.

She dialled the midwife's number. It rang out. Then she redialled and started again. Another twenty seconds of time-out ringing. Callie disguised her panic. 'I think I'll scrub that and ring

Cam. Maybe the midwife is driving and can't answer. That could well be it.'

Fortunately he picked up on two rings. 'What's up?'

'Don't panic,' she told him, 'but Ginny says the baby's on the way. I'm trying to call the midwife but there's no answer. What should I do now?'

The pause told her this first-time father was just about to have a dose of the first-timer jitters on max setting. 'Listen, Cam, you have to be calm. For both of you. And the baby.'

'Okay. Try calling her again. And if there's still no answer, there's another number. It's in Ginny's antenatal file. They said if we couldn't get hold of Dana, we should try the other line. It's an emergency line.'

'Got it. I'll do that. Can you come back? Everything okay?'

'They're taking their time but they're leaving. I'll be there as soon as I can.'

'Please try not to have an accident. We've enough drama without more piling up.'

Cam answered shortly, 'I'll do my best. I'll drive extra-carefully. But tell PookieBuns that I'm going to be there as soon as I can.'

* * *

When Callie found the folder and called the other number, she got the attention she craved. Midwife Dana was tied up in an emergency delivery on the other side of the glen, so another midwife called April would be sent to the estate. Callie told them that there was no way she'd be able to get Ginny into a hospital that was over a hundred miles away now, and given they had protesters and evacuating settlement prospectors, the timing wasn't ideal as the roads were backed up.

It took April twenty-five minutes to send word that she was stuck in her car in traffic that wouldn't move. And there was still no sign of Cam. Callie wanted to go down to the gate, talk to the protesters or even find the police, but she daren't leave Ginny, who was now lying on the floor and panting with exertion.

'Is she here yet?' Ginny asked between short breaths, her face flushed and the hope in her voice suggesting she was desperate for her midwife mentor to appear as soon as possible.

Callie struggled to keep her tone lighter than she felt. 'She's coming. She's called the police to let them know to let her through.' No point in damning this young mother's hope. She'd rather err on the side of optimism, even if she used white lies. 'They'll be clearing the road now so she can get here.'

'I think,' said Ginny, 'that after so much complaining from me about waiting for baby's arrival, this little one has taken its cue to speed things up. Ever delivered a baby before, Callie?'

Callie felt the blood drain from her brain and rallied to keep calm and focused. 'Um, no. But I did see kittens being born once. It happened behind the sofa before we knew what was happening.'

'If a cat can do it behind a sofa, I'm sure we'll be fine,' said Ginny with more composure than Callie felt. Her senses were spinning and her thoughts jangled in her brain as the reality of the moment reared large as life before her.

'This is way bigger than kittens, Gin.'

'Get towels — isn't that what they say in the films? Upstairs cupboard. And hot water. I don't know what comes next . . . ' Ginny flinched as a fresh contraction overtook her and stopped further discourse.

Callie ran for the laundry closet at breakneck speed. She was ultra-keen to get a baby-delivery professional in, and was thinking about using her phone to urge Hamish and Cam to get here fast as well, but she had too much on her hands to do it. She could do nothing except cope with the present moment, even when her thoughts leapt to wondering why the baby had picked that very crucial moment to arrive, choosing the gold-seekers' exit for its own dramatic entry into the world. She imagined they'd tell that story at length for years to come.

She grabbed the towels. She had a very bad feeling about what lay ahead.

★ ★ ★

Cam's voice was clipped and loaded with gravity. 'I can't get through, Callie. Don't tell Ginny in case she panics, but I'm stuck here. A struggle erupted at the settlement and they started a fire. There's a huge blaze now, and it's bad.'

'Should I call the fire brigade?'

Her phone suddenly went dead and Callie stared at it. Cam had told her not to tell his wife about what was happening. She'd never felt more conflicted.

Ginny let out a low moan beside her. She lay on a sheet on blankets and was propped up with all the cushions Callie had been able to find. She'd helped Ginny undress and got her into a nightie. And now she had another crisis on the horizon. She swiftly dialled the emergency services to be on the safe side, with fingers that shook so badly she had to redial. The pregnant woman in labour was now her number-one priority.

She washed her hands again for the umpteenth time and then returned to Ginny. 'You're doing so well, Gin. That's Cam saying he'll be here in a jiffy. I can see your baby's head. I think it's time.'

Ginny groaned. 'I want to push. I really want to push. I'm going to *have* to push.'

Callie took the plunge and went with her instinct. 'I think you should do it. Your body is telling you to, so let's go for it.' She took her friend's hand. 'Remember the antenatal classes. They taught you to how breathe and push.'

Callie needed the midwife. She needed Cam. But right now all they had was each other. And both of them would pull out all the stops for the new heir of Arrach Dean Craig.

Just then Mrs. King, the housekeeper, appeared in the doorway, and the look on her face told Callie she was shocked by her discovery.

'Midwife not here. Ginny can't wait,' Callie told her. 'Have you had much experience with babies?'

'I have four sisters. I was birthing partner to them all.'

'Thank goodness for that,' Callie breathed. But the baby was already arriving and she held out her hands to deliver it, feeling the surge of precious, rare joy that only witnessing a new life brought into the world could bring.

'Looks like you've done a grand job without me.' Mrs. King grinned at her. 'We'll make a midwife stand-in of you yet. Congratulations, Virginia. It's a bouncing baby boy. The new heir is here, and he's as bonnie a lad as we could have hoped for.'

*   *   *

They put Ginny to bed with her new bundle. While they did so, Callie heard the buzz of an aircraft circling above them. It wasn't until Ginny had been dealt with that Callie caught sight of the turmoil on the grounds. She watched dozens of people lying, coughing and shaking on the estate's front lawn. No longer greedy gold-rush opportunists; just people who'd escaped a blaze, blackened and wracked with coughing and shock.

'Oh my goodness,' Callie breathed.

Even the air was smoky with the distant fire. The fire had clearly escalated to a shocking degree. A helicopter now took the neediest on board. Callie saw that the gates to the estate were finally opening to admit an ambulance and a car, which she assumed might well be April the midwife.

Callie's attention went back to the afflicted on the lawn. One young man, barely out of his teens by the looks of him, had blood on his jacket and a face blackened with soot. He'd no doubt come here dreaming of a bright, rich future, but had been left burned and scarred.

All she could think of was, what if things had gone wrong with Ginny? What if prospectors had lost their lives today? What if they'd all had to live with the consequences? And what were the consequences of dreaming of a golden future with Hamish? Was she equally deluded? Did she have no permit for hope? Should she evacuate and retreat?

It was all way too big to take in. The raw emotional void inside her was a dark place she avoided confronting at all costs. But she needed to wake up and step out of her crazy dream.

11

A large helicopter rose noisily over the estate grounds, hovering before it circled in the sky and flew away. Shading her eyes, Callie watched it slowly disappear from view. The injured prospectors would get the medical attention they needed. But her nerves were shot with the rigours of the day. Was everything going into freefall today?

April the midwife had indeed arrived, and was now attending to Ginny and the baby. Mrs. King caught Callie's elbow. 'You look peaky. I think you need tea, dear. Come with me.' Callie nodded. 'Thank you for all you did to help them. Difficult circumstances all round.'

Callie had to work to keep her emotions under control. She suddenly felt ultra-weepy and weak. She'd brought a baby into the world — a new young life like she craved for herself, and it brought her reality starkly to the fore.

'What if there had been complications?' she whispered.

'Don't think of that. It was a straightforward birth. You did all the right things. Your friend will be forever grateful.'

Two burly policeman got out of a police car on the grounds outside, and it all felt a bit too little too late. The protesters were leaving, the smell of burning still tinging the air after the stark drama that had unfolded. And Callie felt a deep void of sorrow engulf her. She was happy for Ginny. But somehow she just wanted out now. Her emotions went into freefall as she sat down in the kitchen, a mug of tea in her hands courtesy of Mrs. King. The tears sprang freely.

Soon April joined her. 'Ginny and the baby are fine,' she assured Callie, 'thanks to you. And the other people will get the medical help they need.'

'I hope so.'

'It's the shock. You'll recover later.'

Should she wait here for Hamish, for his tender arms and care? Should she let herself cry and be comforted by others, even though her usual instinct was to survive, be staunchly independent and push through? Could she summon enough reserves to play stoic in-control Callie and keep her feelings battened down? Ginny's pained expression during her contractions kept plaguing her mind.

She knew now with deep certainty she couldn't stand to let Hamish get any deeper than he'd already burrowed into her inner sanctum. She couldn't give him a happy future or a family. And she could barely keep the deep hurt and heartfelt sorrow at that from breaking her apart. She'd never felt more conflicted. The instinct to flee made her palms damp, it was so powerful, and she itched to make a move before Hamish should appear at the gates in his car. Her thoughts churned as she began to plan what she would do next. Her mind buzzed with confusion and her emotions boiled uncomfortably.

'Do you honestly think she'll be okay?' she whispered to April.

'Of course. Some women do give birth without midwives in attendance, you know. She's just lucky she had you.' April clutched her hands. 'Don't let this situation put you off. Most births go pretty much to plan. No reason to think yours won't go like clockwork when it happens.' She smiled, but Callie couldn't return the gesture. The midwife's assumption hurt her too much. Callie knew she'd likely never be in this situation herself. She was happy and delighted for the Hendersons and their new family, but couldn't stop the tears from streaming fast now in a tell-tale flood. Her chest shuddered with sobs as she tried and failed to self-soothe and save face.

April hugged her. 'You're in a state. That fire has left you in shock.'

But it wasn't just the fire's severity that had her reeling. It was the realisation that her trust had been shattered in her earlier life with her father, along with her faith in her future. Her inability to cope now reminded her of her own inadequacies.

'I'm fine. Just shaken.'

April commented, 'This is usually a sleepy Highland backwater where nothing happens. We've seen it all today.'

A text sounded on Callie's phone in her pocket, and when she scanned it she saw Hamish telling her he couldn't wait to see her; that he'd been having big thoughts about 'future plans'. The day before, she'd have excitedly texted back, but now she had cold feet. And she couldn't face more revelations or soul-searching. Revisiting the wreckage of her own battered future was the last thing she needed.

A memory of her responsibility-shy father climbed the walls in her brain, reminding her of how unfair life could be. She'd never treat a child with such indifferent selfishness. Pretending she had a future with Hamish was equally selfish. So she'd quietly sneak back to her real life and her real issues, without giving Hamish more cause to dream.

'I'm worried about you. Why not have a rest if you can?' April said softly beside her, searching her face.

Callie nodded, and after squeezing her hand April went back to check on Ginny and her baby. Certainty of her course of action sounded inside Callie's brain like a death knell as she walked. It was time to go. She'd worry about dealing with Hamish and his family later. It was time to make decisive moves.

You have to leave. You have to break this off. You can't do this.

She couldn't let herself love this man who already had too much of a hold on her heart. She had to let him go. She might feel like she was dying inside, but she knew what needed to be done. She needed to leave here. And the sooner the better.

Callie walked up to her room and began packing on autopilot, barely registering what she was doing as she folded and stuffed things in her bag. Then she swiftly dressed to leave. Her arrival had been a surprise to Hamish, and she'd leave without his knowledge. He needed to move on and lead his life, and that was the nub of it.

She quietly walked towards the stairs, then backtracked to collect her borrowed phone charger from Hamish's room. Spotting it next to a socket, she glanced at his bedside table. Then she stopped and leaned over to take a closer look, not expecting evidence of his intervention with her business right in front of her: a legal letter with detailed information about the market value of the café. She felt her heart pound in her ears as her fingers held the page to read it better. There was a report on the implications of the new hotel planned nearby, and documents pertaining to its purchase. Why would Hamish have this?

Callie gasped as she read. The papers referred to the new business moving in near hers. The purchaser was identified as a J. Dewar, and the date was recent. Had Hamish been in on this? Was he angling to buy her business all along? And J. Dewar — what interest could her father have in St. Andrews? Puzzlement, shock and smarting disappointment swirled inside her, but no way was she up for recriminations and accusations with the man she'd just vowed to escape.

Setting her lips in determination, she snatched up the paper. She knew taking the documents was wrong but didn't care, needing time to compute the implications. In the end she decided to just take the top sheet, then ran fast down the stairs, hoping to avoid seeing anyone. She'd walk to the nearest village for a taxi or dial one on the way. She didn't want to see Hamish again, not now that she was still processing his behaviour. Why was he digging into her business behind her back?

'The dream wouldn't work, Hamish. I should've remembered that and kept my heart safe in the first place.'

* * *

Hamish couldn't believe what had happened at the settlement when he learned of the evacuation fire. Cam's issues had been dealt with, but in a dramatic and unnecessarily detrimental fashion.

He intended to go back and lay his heart's truths open for Callie. One mission had been accomplished, albeit with more upheaval and harm than they'd ever have wished. Now his most vital personal assignment had to take priority. He'd demonstrate how good Callie made him feel and how he needed her in his life. And seeing Ginny and Cam so happy together galvanised him to seize his chance.

He even had images of their future: rings, proposals, babies in due course. Okay, Callie had said she didn't want children, but in time maybe she'd change her mind. He wanted and craved those things with a ferocity that tore deep. And he wanted them to marry as soon as she'd let him make arrangements. It didn't matter whether it was a big ceremony or just them and two witnesses; he'd take whatever Callie chose. As long as he could make her his wife.

Only one thing jarred: he had to get back to St. Andrews and properly investigate the buyer of The Caddy's Cask Hotel and Bistro. His lawyer-friend's document of discoveries preyed on his mind. Donald MacGregor, law-school friend and St. Andrews property-law specialist, had a tipoff about Callie's competitor. The name J. Dewar in the email now rang alarm bells. He hadn't appreciated the business with Callie's dad. Was J. Dewar a coincidence? Callie had never opened up to him about these private matters before, nor had Linley ever divulged anything.

In other circumstances he'd figure maybe Callie could be expanding her business — but why use a J. in her name? And if something had made Don MacGregor get in touch with a warning, he had to follow it up. Could his friend's hunch have substance? Especially given Callie's revelation that she longed to let the café go. He'd have to warn her about his discovery. But he'd been selfish in guarding this special time together, and he didn't want to start feuds without full facts. Dewar was a popular Scottish name, right? Now that he was buying the café, he had a right to burrow beneath.

Not wanting to wait any longer to speak to her, Hamish took out his phone and dialled her number. The call rang out and clicked to voicemail. He jabbed it again with the same result.

The door of her room stood slightly ajar when he ran up the stairs at Arrach Dean Craig. Still she hadn't answered when he called out to her.

'Callie?' Something, gut instinct probably, twisted in his belly. Hamish stood stock-still and quiet. His instinct was more highly tuned when he closed all else down. Sensing that something was off, he froze when he saw her empty room, with all her clothes gone. It was a blank Callie-free canvas that had his inner sensors on red alert.

'Callie?' He dived at the bathroom door and knocked, but there was no answer. He tried the handle, then went inside and scanned for signs of her. Nothing. 'Callie?'

He went to find Mrs. King. When he eventually located her and asked after Callie, she was as puzzled by her absence as he was. She seemed a bit flustered by his look of panic. 'We've heard from the hospital,' she added. 'All the injured fire victims are now stable.'

'Of course you'll have no idea that Callie delivered Baby Henderson before the midwife got here. She saved the day. I suppose you missed it in all the to-ings and fro-ings?'

'Callie's a special woman, all right. I need to find her. When was she last here?'

Mrs. King looked alarmed at his agitation. He felt sorry for the woman, given that she'd had quite a day with Ginny's surprise delivery. But the fact that Callie hadn't communicated where she'd gone churned inside him.

'Sorry, but I'm worried about her,' he said. 'I'll go and check in case she's left me a note in my room. She could be outside.' And yet his gut told him she wasn't, and that twisted his brain into a tight ball of angst.

He sprinted upstairs. At the door of his room he spotted the last page of his letter about the café and the new hotel's property purchase. It had delivered full information about the property and featured purchaser insights. The letter's final page lay fallen to the floor, which indicated someone had read it.

'Why won't you trust in me, Callie?' he said aloud. She didn't have the knowledge that he'd only been making friendly enquiries via a contact, not meddling in her affairs and private life. Damn it. 'Don't bail on me, Cal!'

But he already knew with dawning certainty that it was all too late. Where on earth had she gone? And this time, had he lost her for good?

★   ★   ★

Callie stood at the train station, waiting for the attendant to finish his phone call so she could ask about tickets and schedules. She was conflicted about what to do. She'd made the decision to leave Hamish, but now that she'd done it she rued her haste.

He'd be angry. Sad. Hurt. All the above and more. He didn't deserve her shabby treatment, born in the fire of anger and her conflicted feelings. Now that she'd had time to think, she questioned her assumptions. The paperwork seemed more an inquiry than a partnership agreement. Something a friend would undertake? She felt wretched about herself, sorry about acting in haste and pique. But would Hamish see it that way? Probably not.

243

She should have left him a note. But too late — she was on her way to Spean Bridge, then to Ballachulish to retrieve Violet, and back to Fife from there.

She couldn't turn back now. Backdowns had never been her strong point. That much she'd inherited from her father, to her cost. Her campervan was kaput in Ballachulish, but she hoped that would soon be sorted. She'd no reason to return to Spean Bridge, but she still had the key and had left a couple of things there, including a bracelet of her mother's. Stupid that she'd left it, but she blamed it on Hamish's haste. Other than that, all she'd left was a small amount of washing, and she could do without it. The bracelet not so much. She could probably just call Fraser about the van and tell him she'd decided to head back to Fife, but leaving the precious heirloom behind bothered her.

As it happened, fate had other ideas.

'Callie. It's me.'

She whirled around, surprised the

male voice wasn't Hamish's. 'Fraser. What are you doing here?'

'I'm visiting a friend and fetching your car part. I said I'd drop in a package at the station as an errand on my way back.'

'Wow, that's some coincidence. It's so remote here.'

'Remote' was a flattering description. She'd never seen a station so out of the way. It was just tracks and a shed and a tumbleweed-style vista with hills in the far, far distance.

'I often do pick-ups and delivery jobs for extra cash. And picking up a part for your van on the way made it more economical. It's in my car. Listen, can I take you somewhere? Where's your friend with the grumpy manner?'

'He had urgent business,' Callie lied. She felt bad about that, but it was so much easier than telling the truth, and anyway Fraser didn't need to know. But something bothered her about him. He scanned the horizon as if he was checking for something.

'Are you okay, Callie? You look upset.'

I'm fine. You okay yourself?' she asked.

'I'm great. Listen, I'm going back to Ballachulish. Do you want a lift? Crazy not to ride along. I'll get you there faster than the train.'

She hesitated. Some crazy instinct told her that this coincidence was just a bit too creepy. But her need to avoid Hamish also screamed that she was in a fix and not to look a gift horse in the mouth. 'Okay. But let me pay for petrol.'

'Don't be silly. There's no need. As I said, this is me doing several jobs at once.'

'But I need to pay you for the campervan work. It's likely I'm heading home next, and I'll have to come back and fetch the van.'

'All right, I agree about sharing the bill. But no need to disappear. Hang around at the pub and I'll get the van working for you. Or I could even get it sorted at the cottage if you want.'

'Really? You don't mind? I left something at the cottage I'd love to retrieve, so a quick stop there would be ideal.'

'I have the part, so as soon as we're back I'll get onto it.' He smiled, and the sincere light in his eyes calmed some of the fears that nagged inside Callie's mind. Relief surged through her for the first time in hours.

'Great!' she said. She'd be able to pick up her bracelet and clothes, and then she'd be on her way. 'You've been a lifesaver yet again, Fraser. I'm really, really grateful.'

He grinned at her. 'We never did get a chance to share lunch. But a journey, in my book, is just as good. I enjoy your company. Lady luck has shone on us today. Maybe I'll persuade you into having dinner later?'

She felt herself groan inwardly. Yes, she'd sorted out her predicament, but she recognised how deflated she felt that Fraser just could not ever take a hint. It contrasted sharply with how she'd felt about going away with Hamish. How things had worsened. And she felt the tender zones of her heart at their impasse.

Her silence must have given Fraser an answer. 'Let's get in the car and head off back then,' he said.

12

Back at Bracken Cottage, Callie invited Fraser in, but he declined. She saw him retrieve a box from the rear of his car and take out his phone, then dial someone. She felt too relieved to know she'd soon be heading home to worry about the fact she was back here without Hamish. What was done was done. Now she had to see it fully through.

'I'm going to call my mate Dave to bring the van,' Fraser said. 'He has a tow truck. That okay?'

'Sure. Why don't I make us tea?' She could murder one herself, so was only too pleased to help him speed up in his work via tea motivation.

'Sounds perfect. Dave'll be here soon.'

As she went upstairs, Callie heard his familiar voice but couldn't distinguish the words. It sounded like a terse conversation, perhaps an argument. Maybe Dave was less than happy to have a job thrust upon him without warning. But she figured that was Fraser's affair. He was kind, but he'd also been hard going, quizzing her on way too many things on the way back, from her marital status to all about Hamish, and she'd figured that really was none of his business. He'd seemed very interested in Hamish's aunt too.

She retrieved her bracelet, immensely grateful to have it back in her possession, and stuffed it back in her pocket. Now all that remained was to collect her washing from where she'd left it on the towel rail.

She sensed him before she saw him. Standing tall. Too close. 'Fraser. What is it?'

'You haven't worked it out yet?'

'What do you mean?'

The bathroom suddenly felt way too small. His expression told of his intent before his low threat sounded. 'You walked right into this one. Just glad you saw sense and ditched the boyfriend before I had to take action on him myself.' His large, rough hand grasped her wrist and it hurt.

'What are you doing?' Callie cried.

'Putting you somewhere you can't get in the way.' He yanked her and she felt her bones jar.

'What is this?'

'You. You're surplus. I don't want you calling unwelcome visitors with sirens and stripes.'

He pushed her round roughly against the wall. Her head bumped against the rough plaster and he pinioned the back of her leg with his knee to keep her there. Meanwhile, he frisked her pockets. She felt his hand glide over the bracelet and he took it out, examined it, then rammed it back so roughly she felt it hurt through the denim of her jeans. 'Money's in my bag,' she managed to say.

'I don't want your money or your old ratty jewels. I have bigger plans. But I need your phone.'

'It's downstairs too.'

She wished she had it. She also knew there was a panic alarm in her handbag. And what was the point of it being in there when the one awful moment in her life had come, and she was being attacked now and held against her will — in rural Scotland, with nobody for miles to hear and help?

'So I'm guessing the campervan thing was a lie,' she gasped.

'Sold already. Got me a nice price. You were way too easy. The number plate fetched a tidy sum too.'

Sharp tears sprung into Callie's eyes, but she vowed not to let them fall. 'Nice line in hospitality you have going there.'

'I'm about to lose the pub. I need bail-out money. You came along at the perfect time.'

Callie wished she had the strength to push him off and kick him somewhere painful, but he was much taller and stronger than she was. She wouldn't stand a chance.

He grabbed both of her wrists and pushed her ahead of him. 'So let's just say you're going for a little enforced break. Somewhere quiet, with a dead-bolt. Think of it as a little unexpected holiday. A reward for good behaviour.'

'Right. Forgive me if I don't thank you.'

He pushed her ahead of him down the stairs, and her legs shook like saplings in a strong wind. Before she knew it, he opened the under-stairs cupboard that had no light but was deep and long enough for her to stay in without discomfort; and yes, she knew there was a lock there — one on the outside. The cupboard stored skis and outdoor garden equipment. And now it had new company: her. Karma for her treatment of Hamish? Reward for her poor judgement and bad behaviour?

'Let's just say when I visited the other day I got a good idea what this place had to offer,' Fraser said. 'And there's plenty of stuff stashed here. Antiques. Silver. Never mind a cellar with a lot of wine stashed that some collectors may find a good use for.'

'I should've guessed you were only out for money.'

He sniffed, and his voice had a cruel and calculating rasp when he spoke. 'Nice fittings — silver cutlery, candelabras on the dining table, and plenty more in the cupboards besides what's on offer at first glance. I knew as soon as I saw the paintings — expensive tastes, and I know people who will fetch me a good price. It'll all stack up. It was my lucky day when you walked into the bar. You had no idea how lucrative you could be. I'd figured I'd just sell your old van for scrap, so this is a happy event. Call it a windfall if you like.'

It made Callie's stomach churn to think of Flora receiving the news that her precious sanctuary had been ripped off under her watch. She felt like a fool to have brought all this upon them. Why had she been so ready to trust a stranger when she wouldn't trust Hamish, who she'd known all her life?

'I intend to milk this place for all it's worth,' Fraser carried on. 'You see if I don't!'

'You think so, do you?' said a grim male voice from the door that stopped him in his tracks. 'Leave the woman alone — and forget your big idea of nicking everything of any value from this place. The police have been called and you're busted, laddie. We don't take kindly to chancers who think they can rip off our own! We're Highlanders with hearts in these parts.'

Crouched, shaking and crying in the cupboard hole Fraser had pushed her into, Callie had never been so grateful for surprise visitors in her life. Agnes Drysdale and her husband had arrived with perfect timing. The woman who had so kindly fed Hamish and herself on their first night had now stepped in to stop a burglary on Flora's property. Callie would be forever in their debt.

A siren sounded and she sensed Fraser make a run for it, bursting out of the door past his elderly assailants

— though from the shouts and tussle noises outside, she assumed he hadn't got far.

'Are you okay, lassie?' The small voice of Agnes Drysdale reached her in her unwelcome prison. Callie felt like she'd backed into her tightest, darkest corner yet.

'No,' she answered. 'It's all my fault. All of it. I deserve what almost happened.'

'Sshh. There now, girlie. It's going to come out right in the end. You've helped get a baddie into a cell, for starters. And it's only money. Flora will be more mortified at what's happened to you. You've some hideous bruises, if you don't mind me saying.'

'Thank God you came when you did,' said Callie, sliding down to the floor. She felt the bracelet in her pocket snap, but she was too overcome not to fall. She deserved this. She'd treated Hamish terribly, and she was the one who'd brought trouble to Bracken Cottage's door.

Was everything in her life destined to

mess up? She let go and finally gave way to sobbing. Trouble just kept finding her.

*   *   *

She awoke in a rushed panic, grabbing at her neck to remove the remembered pressure of Fraser's grasping fingers. She recoiled and struggled to breathe — then swiftly realised she was safe and recalled Alec Drysdale standing in the doorway with his wife Agnes behind, staring in utter shock.

Callie collapsed against the bed frame and focused on her breath as she surveyed the room she lay in. From the tea station and fire-escape signs posted on the wall, she knew she had to be in bed-and-breakfast hell. But it was far preferable to the realisation of what could have happened to her at Fraser's hands. What had he intended to do with her after he'd got what he wanted? Would she still be alive now had he succeeded?

Agnes and Alec, Highland vigilantes,

had cajoled her into staying with them at Rowan Byres Hotel. She felt like a fugitive, with only a rucksack to her name. She was glad she hadn't tried to stay overnight in Flora's cottage. Just the thought of returning there for her remaining few belongings gave her hives. She wasn't sure if that was due to the thwarted robbery or the threat of Hamish arriving when she least expected.

This new day brought a whole new perspective and a head full of assorted wonders and regrets. Mostly regrets at what she'd done. Reality trickled into her memory — she'd walked out on Hamish, but she'd also seen evidence that he was up to no good, and was maybe even in league with her father. Could that be true? Could the J. Dewar developing St. Andrews's latest boutique hotel be her long-absent dad? And why was Hamish sending lawyer enquiries about her business interests anyhow? She thought she'd been clear that she wouldn't take his offer. Was he out to shaft her?

She sighed. But that wasn't the main reason she'd bailed. She'd scared herself witless about how she should confide her medical bombshell. Hamish deserved the entire truth, but that was a place she wasn't prepared to go. Admitting to wanting a family with a man you'd spent half your life loving from afar was a new league of 'awkward meets impossible to solve'. He wanted her — but he most likely wanted the dream-Callie who could give him all the things he wanted from his life. The Callie she'd once thought she could be.

She'd pleaded with Agnes not to call Flora or Hamish, and to give her time to return back to St. Andrews without fuss. The only real damage done in this instance was the campervan theft, and Callie was prepared to take that on the chin.

She washed and dressed, noting the tired lines beneath her eyes — not to mention the sharp pains in her heart. She'd gone downstairs to the hotel kitchen when a familiar voice made her imitate a statue. Dreading confrontation and trying not to move, she held her breath.

'So no one has seen her?' Hamish's stern voice drifted from the reception area. Callie's innards clenched into a wire tangle at the recognition.

Agnes staunchly replied, 'It's as if she vanished into thin air, lad. I've asked all the guests, and I phoned around the village after you called last night. You must take care to calm down, lad. She'll come out in her own time. Hell hath no fury . . . '

'I can't calm down. She's out there, with no transport or place to go. I couldn't stand to think of her sleeping rough or getting lost and coming to harm. Maybe she's lying hurt somewhere.'

The moisture in Callie's mouth had dried up. She pinned down the need to gasp and kept herself mute by force.

'Lovers' tiffs can be like that,' Agnes opined. 'Love's young dream one minute; dragons baying for blood the next.'

Hamish's terse mental state was easy

to discern in his ground-out words. 'There was no tiff. It has to be a misunderstanding.'

'She's a grown and resilient woman, my lad. Maybe try the hostel up in Glentiel?'

'I'll do that. Any other suggestions?'

'Calm down. She'll come to you when she wants to.'

'Well if she comes here, please tell her I know about it all. I know about the attack at Bracken Cottage and what happened. If she's worried that anybody's angry at her, she doesn't need to be. I'm only concerned about her safety and her welfare. I don't know why she left me, but be sure to tell her I'm worried sick. I care about her.'

Agnes paused, and for a moment Callie considered stepping out and confronting him, if only because his words caused guilt so intense she couldn't bear to stand there holding her breath while he said kind things about her.

But Agnes stopped her taking action

by restarting the conversation. 'I'm the community council chair, and the first port of call for most things, so if the lass is around these parts I'm sure to get wind of it.'

'All I want is to know that she's safe.' Hamish's gruff response almost made Callie reconsider and walk out to face the music, but guilt and fear held her back. She'd never considered herself an out-and-out coward before this moment. Agnes and Hamish continued their conversation, but she struggled to hear it over the rapid loud beating of her own heart in her ears. Then she heard the door shut and Agnes appeared, her face drawn.

'So sorry you're in the middle of this, lass,' she said. 'Anyway, he's gone. And may the good Lord forgive me for breaking his holy commandments.'

Callie put her hand over her mouth. 'You lied for me. I'm so sorry.'

'It's fine, my dear. I lie all the time when I tell drunk guests that the bar is shut when it isn't and they're too gone to know better. I've even been known to change the clock.'

Alec came in. 'He drove off,' he said. 'Go on now to the kitchen and eat up some of that breakfast. I'll get you to the station in good time for your train.'

'You've both been so kind.' Callie heard the hitched wavering note in her voice that threatened tears. But she vowed to be strong.

Alec grinned, then gallantly bowed. 'Positive regard without judgement comes on the house. Agnes and I used to indulge in a fair bit of the argy-bargy when we were winching, but we always made up in the end. Enjoy some breakfast — you need something inside you, lass, to settle the nerves.'

In the kitchen, Callie discovered a wooden table laden with porridge, scrambled eggs, bacon, and orange juice.

'Food heals the soul — Alec will take you to the station when you're done,' said Agnes.

'I'll repay all your kindness and more.'

'No need, lass. We rally to help those in need in these parts. Life would be a dismal place if nobody reached out to help a traveller in despair.'

Callie immediately thought of Ginny and wondered about her baby. It almost made her cry. She took her phone from her pocket and scanned it. So far today she'd ignored all of Hamish's texts. Seeing Ginny's message to her, she said softly, 'He's now named Hamish Cameron Henderson.'

Yet despair swirled inside her. She'd loved Hamish before she'd even been a woman herself. Finding him and losing him was the most awful experience of her entire life — worse even than what Fraser had done. She'd just found heaven, then worked out she wasn't allowed in. In the last few days she'd woken up to the fact that her life was a sham and her world was falling apart.

'He'll get over it, and so will I,' she told herself, without believing it. She was only battening down the necessary conviction with iron chains. She had to move on — even though, while she bled inside, she pretended her heart was made of stone.

★　★　★

Callie's phone rang, and she saw from the status bar that there had already been a series of texts, emails and calls in the last few minutes. She pressed the 'receive' button as the countryside flashed by her train. Linley's name was stark on her phone screen.

'Why haven't you picked up?' Linley's voice accused, sounding aggrieved. 'Ten texts last night. All ignored. And the landline at the cottage is never answered.'

'Sorry. What's up?' Did Linley think she was the only woman in St. Andrews allowed a private life?

'Do you have any idea where Hamish is?'

Did this mean Linley wasn't part of Flora's plan? Did she know about the double-booking? Too many questions. 'He's your brother. Why are you asking me? I haven't seen him since he walked out after our row.' Big fat lie of the day. But discussing Hamish with his sister was the last thing she wanted right now.

'I've been trying to get him. No answer. I'm desperate, so thought I'd ask you.'

'He's left my employment, so it's none of my concern.'

But Linley's brevity and tone told Callie that this was far from a courtesy call. 'I'm calling because it's urgent. And this has implications for you.'

Callie went silent. Something inside her stomach unfurled like a plume of foreboding smoke.

'You've a cousin arrived from Auckland,' Linley said. 'Jenny Dewar. She's here in St. Andrews wanting to meet you and planning to stay. She's a chef hotelier and the purchaser of the new hotel. She's married but she kept her maiden name because she's so well known. Imagine, Callie — your competition is family. She couldn't be nicer, too.'

'You can't be right,' Callie muttered. 'There must be some mistake.'

'Jenny is the new owner of The Caddy's Cask Hotel and Bistro, and she's dying to meet you. Her father emigrated after serving in the navy, and the family lost touch. She has big plans for the place, as her husband is golf-crazy and this is his dream project. I don't think she'll be out to compete with your business at all.'

The breath stalled in Callie's throat as she sat with the handset stuck to her head but her fingers numb and her heart thudding. Maybe Hamish wasn't out to hatch plans against her. Maybe she'd assumed the worst, and been spectacularly wrong.

'I'm on my way back now, Lin,' she said. 'I'll be back by this afternoon.'

'I told Jenny she can stay with me until you get here, but she's got a suite booked at the big golf hotel that costs mega bucks — they're loaded. She's lovely, Cal. You're going to adore her when you get together. She'll breathe new life into the city, never mind your life. The new hotel may not be the downer you've imagined after all.'

Callie's emotions whirled. Surprise mixed with shock, remorse, and foolishness. She'd thought that after Gramps's passing, she'd lost family links for good. She remembered clearly when her dad had gone and Gramps had to explain that he wasn't coming back, and they carried on like normal, hardly talking about it. Only now someone cared enough about the legacy to opt back in.

'I still need to find Hamish,' said Linley. 'It's important. Strasbourg have called — they have an urgent opening. He needs to deal with this a.s.a.p., but I don't want him to leave, Cal. You have to try and help me make him stay.'

When it came to Hamish, Callie was determined to never involve herself again. The doors were sealed, the windows taped over. Never could she let her emotions betray her, and the best way to ensure that would be to keep him firmly at bay, out of the danger zone.

'Can't help, sorry,' she said. 'I think that's a family issue, don't you? Tell Jenny I'm coming back soon, please, and I'm looking forward to meeting her. I hope you find Hamish — he really should be back doing what he does best. You'll all help him work out what that is, I'm sure of it.'

★ ★ ★

Callie was surrounded by the hubbub of her café, but she only had eyes for her cousin, Jenny Dewar. The aroma of freshly roasted coffee beans was a balm to past hurts, and the opportunity to drown sorrows with some off-limits pastries beckoned. Jenny enthralled Callie with her charm and natural positivity. She was a rock that Callie badly needed for salvation right now.

'You know,' Jenny told her, 'I get such powerful vibrations in this place. And your aura right now — wow. Powerful emotions at play. Would you like me to do you a reading?'

As much as the statement intrigued Callie, fear of what Jenny might uncover made her decline. Though she sensed they'd have some interesting discussions ahead when she was able to share.

'I can't believe Father never came back here,' said Jenny, sipping tea from Callie's own vintage rosebud teacup. 'And now I wish I'd come sooner. All this history was here and I had no idea.'

'Whatever prompted you to buy the hotel?' Callie asked, genuinely intrigued.

'Actually, we employed a property agent to do the work for us. We said we wanted a restaurant or hotel business in St. Andrews, and when we learned there was a property on the same street that Daddy's ancestors worked on, we went for it. We then researched the family tree in a big way. We'd only seen a video tour from the agent, but bought the property anyway — and now that I'm here, we're delighted. We can build something fabulous, and I love the café even more than the hotel.'

Callie smiled. 'I've worked here all

my life.' She had taken the extreme decision to hire Claude Debeau for a further few days to enable her to come to terms with having a long-lost cousin and get to know her. Jenny was a stunning woman with bright brown eyes and dusty blonde hair in an elfin style. The more they spoke, the more Callie liked her and figured Grandpa would have been proud of her achievements.

Callie inhaled sharply and put her palms flat on the table. Time to be honest. 'I hate to break this to you, but I might be letting the café go soon. As much as it's been a huge part of my life, and I love it — and hate it too at times — I've worked up to the fact that I have dreams I'm not pursuing. I'm owed a chance to explore what I love. So I'm planning to put it up for sale.'

Jenny dropped her cup into its saucer with a clatter. 'You're selling up?'

'If I can find a buyer. It's time for me to stretch my own wings. I only realised lately, but I need to part ways and find a new direction. The café's great, but it's time to make a new start.'

'I don't suppose you'd give me first refusal?'

Callie watched her newfound relative. 'That's a big decision, Jenny. Don't feel you have to offer.'

'Trust me — if I'm buying the hotel and the café is up for grabs, I want the set, no question. Would you sell to me if we formalise things and do it properly?'

Callie gulped. This was it: her big divorce from her past obligations. It wasn't as upsetting as she'd imagined it would be; no lightning from the sky struck her down. 'It would be the answer to both of our desires,' she said. 'So you've a background in the hotel trade?'

Jenny filled her in. She had impressive credentials and loads of awards to her name. 'Michael is the hotelier,' she said, 'and I'm the restaurateur. We've both had failed marriages and want to make a life change. In fact, we want to renew our vows soon with a Scottish ceremony — I'm thinking a castle and kilts. Being here will be the best of both worlds. It's Michael's passion for golf that's brought us; the ancestry part was the thing that helped tick all the boxes.'

The roar of a motorbike sounded up the street outside the café. Callie knew the sound of that engine without seeing it and she swallowed hard. A feeling of doom dawned inside her ribcage as her heart pounded. She'd managed to avoid Hamish and his phone messages and texts, and ban him from her brain since her escape. But now she sensed she'd have to face the music. And the brass band was beating the big drum outside.

'Look, Jenny,' she said, 'do you think we could meet again tomorrow lunch-time? My treat somewhere nice?'

'Sure, that'd be fabulous. And remember, I'm serious about the café purchase. Get onto your lawyer and we'll get things finalised.'

Rather than have a scene inside, Callie walked Jenny out to bid her farewell. Ironic that she was going to have to face the man who'd first suggested she sell up.

Having parked his bike, Hamish came up to her and removed his helmet, revealing a grim-faced gritty readiness to talk. 'Callie. You want to go out back or something?'

'No. I don't have much to say to you. And if you've come to lecture me about your aunt's near robbery, then don't. I feel bad enough already, so nothing you say can make it worse.'

'Nothing was further from my mind. I was scared witless you weren't okay. In common with my aunt, all we care about is your welfare. So you want to argue in the street then?'

'Nope. I don't want to talk. Period. After I saw you were making enquiries in secret about my business behind my back, I lost all interest in anything you have to say.' She didn't watch him, but could feel his presence as he came to stand, leather-and-jeans-clad beside her. 'I made enquiries as a concerned friend only. With your interests at heart. I want a chance to talk to you. It's the mini-mum I deserve.'

'I think we had a lucky reprieve. And we should just agree to leave things be.' Callie could feel customer gazes on her from the café, and Jonty's alert-with-concern face appeared beside the door. She mouthed, 'Do you need help, Cal?'

Callie shook her head and gave her a look of reassurance.

'Callie, let's walk. Please?'

Her stomach knotted, her mouth dried, and everything inside her screamed not to notice the man her brain and her heart craved to watch. His profile, his gaze, his everything. But none of it could ever be. Never. They'd tried and failed.

'You have exactly five minutes,' she said. 'But please don't expect me to back down on anything, because I don't intend to. I'd say I'd friend-zoned you. But I think even that's stretching it. Let's agree to nod in passing and leave it there.'

★ ★ ★

Hamish and Callie stood at the railings near the cathedral ruins, and the whip of the wind slapped them both full in the face. And Callie deserved the nature lash, she figured. She'd hurt Hamish more than he could stand.

'You left,' he began. 'No warning, no reasons, no regard, no apology. That it? That all I deserve? You cut me to the quick, and put yourself in grave danger.' He denied the impact of her fresh-strawberry aroma. He wouldn't let it yank his chain to loving Callie beyond all else.

She flicked him a disdainful look, squared her shoulders, and met his gaze with those blue eyes that had softened when she'd laughed in his arms. 'I left because I can't be what you need. We made a rash mistake promising things to each other. A bit like a holiday romance that doesn't add up to anything when you get back to your real life. I just wish you'd wake up to that.'

'And what makes you qualified to decide all this without my input?'

'Listen, Hamish, we both know you're trained to win arguments. Trust me to know a relationship won't work. Call it instinct. You and I were never a workable plan — we just let your family fool us into kidding ourselves. When I realised you'd been asking questions about the café, I felt invaded. Why didn't you admit it? Were you like Fraser — out to see if I was worth investing in?'

'Don't ever compare me to that creep! I'm so angry about how he stalked you. Do you realise how worried that whole affair made me?' He pushed closer and bit his lower lip. 'At least explain yourself. You bolted from Cameron's without a word. I worried like hell about you for days until Linley told me you were back. I can't believe you'd treat me that way.'

Callie had her hard-as-nails armour on and it spiked him via dismissive daggers with every word. 'You're not listening. I told you. I left because I can't give you what you need. You have dreams of a family, don't you? I can't do futures and families or tie you to my limitations. We have no future, Hamish. When are you going to get that?'

'You don't want a family with me? Or you don't want me?' He couldn't compute her reasoning. They hadn't even talked about that level of future together, and she kept shoving 'no future family' at him. But yes, he did want kids. And in order to have them, he needed her in his life to have them with.

'It's not about not wanting. It's about not being able to have them. Please, stop pushing me to places I don't want to discuss. I can't have children. With you or anyone. Not won't or choose not to — *can't*. The doctor confirms it's as likely as my dad is to care about his past. There. Got it loud and clear yet?'

Hamish saw the glisten of tears in her eyes and felt all his senses reel at the revelation. Her pain was all the harder to see in the taut lines of her face and the pinched look in her mouth. Had

Callie been battling with a set of grim circumstances so huge while he'd been waxing on about futures? It knocked him back on his heels just imagining, and made him itch to explain and apologise.

'Oh Callie, I should never — '

'Stop right there. Let me finish.'

He gulped, nodded, and felt like someone had rammed a bayonet into his flesh. 'I'm sorry. I didn't mean to interrupt. I just need to tell you you're brave and I care how you're feeling. This has been huge for you.'

'Don't be kind or say anything. I didn't want to tell you. Or anyone.' She turned away. 'When I found out you'd been meddling in my business, I realised I was right to be wary. But at heart I always knew that we really cannot work.'

'There you go again, jumping to conclusions. I was worried that there was a nasty surprise in store for the café and wanted to investigate, that was all. The business thing was me protecting your interests because Linley asked me to pull some favours — she knew you were worried about the new development. Why do you assume I'm out to do you harm?'

'Not important. Let's conclude it's all been a lucky escape for us both.'

'A heartbreak and a massive disappointment for me. I can't stop caring about you just because you tell me to.'

Disappointment. That's what I'm saving you from. No kids. No real future. Hard decisions down the line. Callie turned to walk back, but Hamish matched her strides and fell in line, not letting her escape.

'Your reasoning doesn't even add up, Cal.'

Her eyes felt full of unshed tears. Trust Hamish to keep this unwanted conversation on topic. She wished she could explain properly, but she knew if she let go she'd never stop sobbing. She wouldn't emerge out of the vortex of grief for months. He made her sound so cold and callous, when all she'd been trying to do was save him from having his dreams dashed later.

'All I've ever wanted was to be with you,' he said. 'To prove you matter to me. But now I see I've been kidding myself.' Hamish let out a raw gasp of anger. 'Didn't you ever think you matter to me?'

Callie couldn't answer truthfully, not without giving herself away. She looked down at her watch. 'I need to get back.'

'And I thought lawyers were heart-less.'

Raw anger spiked as they stopped and stood toe to toe. 'I have a café to run. The fact that you spied on my business interests was never going to recommend you as a man to trust.'

'Linley and I wanted to protect you. We're on different planets when it comes to trust.'

'Best if we agree to stay out of each other's way. I'm keeping the café firmly in the family and selling soon as I'm able,' she stated firmly.

'Running away I'd say,' Hamish

answered. Then he turned and walked off.

Leaving her lungs heaving with the need to vent and cry. Or to find a bar, order a vile double whisky and try to dull the pain of a raging broken heart.

★   ★   ★

Callie stood in the café's pantry, sobs pulling her insides apart, inch by painful inch. Because the scared and hurt girl inside her cared and loved Hamish back. That girl wanted him more than life itself.

He said he loved her — but she couldn't let him. He said she mattered and he wanted a future — but did he really want to share the future she'd been dealt? Words were easy. But what would happen when his mediocre life with her dragged him into monotony and he yearned for more? What about when a pregnancy didn't materialise? What about when he sought new legal fame? Callie's throat was hoarse with crying. But she knew she'd done the right thing and had to remain strong.

'Cal, you in there? What's up? Let me in.' Jonty rattled the door handle. Thankfully the bolt was in place; Callie couldn't face more questions.

'Be there in a minute.'

'Callie, I'm so worried about you. You're not okay, are you? Don't lie and say yes when I know flipping well you aren't.'

'I'm not okay yet. But I will be, in time.'

But she knew that was optimistic. She'd have to pretend to be okay for a long time to come. She was in a cold store crying about a man she loved but couldn't ever hope for. How much harder could it ever be?

* * *

Flora had made a reservation, and Callie had already baked the maple-glazed Danish pastries she loved the best. The café table setting had been laid with extra care because Flora Gordon was nothing if not precise. But as soon as Callie saw her elderly friend's face, she knew she shouldn't have bothered. Nothing would sweeten this situation, and she was in for a truckload of Gordon trouble. Flora's rigid features and puffing breathing communicated 'upset schoolmarm about to spout steam'.

Then Callie noticed Linley walking down the street, carrying her ultra-expensive patent-leather designer handbag and looking as fresh as a daisy in a yellow twin-set ensemble. Two Gordons for the price of one. All she needed was for Hamish to turn up on the bike and she'd have the hat trick.

Callie wiped her hands and left the kitchen. She greeted her special senior customer herself. 'Flora, what can I get for you today?'

'You can sit your behind down in this chair. I don't care what buns you're baking. We have business to discuss.'

'Hi, Linley,' she greeted her friend, and Linley had the decency to not only nod but look sheepish.

'Do I detect double trouble?'

Flora's imperious look turned in Linley's direction, daring her to respond. Instead, Linley meekly took a seat. Callie felt doom perform an ungainly and poorly trained parachute-jump slap bang into the centre of her unready belly. The situation made her insides squirm awkwardly.

Flora called out, 'Callie, you're joining us. Order us three high teas and we'll get this over with.'

Callie steeled herself to obey, like chief mourner at the state funeral of conscience.

Flora added, 'You get to be this testy when you reach your eighties; it's down in bold in the rule-book of life.'

Callie opted for stonewalling. 'Flora, as much as I appreciate your visit, I can't talk for long; it's a busy shift. I'm in the middle of — '

'Tumshie and bunkum. There are things you need to know. And since Linley and I were both responsible for getting you and Hamish up to that cottage together, I thought we'd both come and lay the facts before you.'

Callie twisted to watch her friend. 'You?'

'At Flora's insistence. I arranged the cottage escape and I helped make it happen. I knew Hamish would be there too,' Linley admitted.

'Your friend status just disintegrated.'

Linley pouted, but her cheeks had a rosy flush. 'Well somebody had to. I thought putting him to work in the café would sort it, but that failed miserably. It's like your potential as a couple just implodes at every opportunity.'

'Ha!' Callie shouted, and some customers looked up sharply at her madness, but Callie no longer cared. 'I knew you set me up on purpose.'

'Well you may as well know that Hamish didn't want to be here. I twisted his arm to force him to help you. Whatever works, eh?'

Callie scowled and shook her head. 'I guess you get your evil side from your relatives.' She'd never taken Flora on before — she wouldn't have dared; but maybe the injustice boulders were too highly stacked to ignore the landslide. Time to fight back with force.

But the look Flora threw her was anger unbridled. And Callie had never had a full-on fight with an octogenarian before. In the Hall of Awkwardness, this was the ultimate wall-sized portrait with a gallery label beneath that said 'Big Bad Awful in Hideous Oils'. Should she leave now, or push it and really cause a memorable stink?

'In view of your plan's failure, let's not talk about Hamish anymore,' Callie said softly. 'This is my café and I don't want a scene. People talk, and you both set me up way above your jurisdiction, so you've no room to negotiate.'

'Hamish's engagement was a sham,' said Linley suddenly. 'I made up that his girlfriend was more than that. I had a photo of them at a party and photoshopped in a ring. I made up the story to see if you'd react, but that didn't work either. You did your usual and internalised and ignored the information. All I'd ever wanted was to get you both together, because my brother is so in love with you he won't move on and find anybody else. Even his ex-girlfriend Allessa realised he was a lost cause and opted to go out with his friend Tom.'

'It's true,' said Flora. 'But we love Hamish. And we love you. You're perfect for each other. And Hamish has never loved anybody else.'

Callie stared and blinked. 'Is this another dramatic ruse to trick me?'

'No,' Flora reprimanded. 'It's a wake-up call to Callie Dewar to stop denying herself the most wonderful man she could ever wish for. You're breaking his heart. And I don't know what happened between you in the Highlands, but it's got to be solvable, surely?' For an elderly Scots lady, Flora had stern prickle enough for a clump of thistles.

'I don't want to discuss it. But just so you know, Hamish isn't as in love with me as you think he is. He might be in love with the idea of me. But he'll want to leave sooner or later. I won't be enough.' *I wasn't enough for Dad to consider staying, either.*

'Listen, lass, little did I know how stubborn you can be,' Flora said, her cheeks shaking and her skin so translucent in places the veins showed like a seniority watermark. The sight pulled Callie up — the woman was her elder, and her motives were merely to promote her nephew's welfare. 'My Hamish would cross hot coals to win you. And all you do is jump to wrong conclusions. You must make amends before it's too late.'

Linley added quickly, 'He's always been in love with you, Cal. It pains me so to think you can't trust in him — or me — enough to accept he means it.'

Flora held out a warning finger. 'I've waited too many years of my life to see him happy to let you mess things up at the final hurdle. What on earth is wrong with you?'

Callie palmed her forehead. Their words drove her crazy. 'He thinks he loves me — but am I really enough? Will he work out I can't compete with his achievements, and get bored?'

'He's packing to leave. I demand you go see him, or he may never come back.' Flora turned and picked up her box of cakes the waiter had brought. Then, her head shaking with anger, she replaced it on the table. 'I can't and won't eat these. You know I've always promoted your cause. But I won't come here again until you remove whatever concrete block in your heart keeps Hamish at bay. Put him out of his misery. All he wants is your future assured, and you're being too cautious to see it.'

Callie rose and prepared to turn her back on two Gordons at once. 'I'm sorry, but I have problems of my own to deal with. I've had recent health news that means I need to re-evaluate my future. So Hamish isn't my priority. I'm sorry, but there's nothing else I can say.'

Linley nailed her with an intense stare and grabbed hold of her arm. 'What's happened?'

'Don't worry; I'm not ill, Lin. We'll talk about it some other time in private, I promise. Once I've got my own feelings in order. For now, all I can manage is to deal with this on my own.'

★ ★ ★

Jonty sidled up to Callie while she was reading a new recipe so intently that she didn't see her approach.

'I need to talk,' the chef said softly, making Callie jump.

'Hi, Jonty. Sure; what's up? Don't tell me we've run out of strawberry tarts again. I'm onto it. I'm just a bit behind.'

Her friend and colleague bit her lip. 'I have news, and not about strawberry tarts. In fact it impacts on you. And work.'

Callie searched her friend's face, and as she did a penny dropped and she pre-empted the words seconds before they were voiced.

Jonty's expression told of bottled-up excitement waiting to pop. 'Mack and I have happy news, and I'm still pinching myself — but before I burst, I wanted to tell you properly. I'd hate for it to get out before we had a chance to talk. We're expecting a baby, due early next year. I wanted to give you ample warning. Do you think it'd be remiss of me to bring it up with your cousin, Jenny?'

'Congratulations! I'm so very pleased for you.' Callie opened her arms to welcome her friend for a hug. She was also pretty impressed with her own calm, collected coping reaction to the news. But she was genuinely pleased for her friend. It had been several years since Jonty and Mack had married, and she'd known deep down it was only a question of time. 'You'll both make wonderful parents,' she said in a rushed breath.

'The thing is, I'd quite like to return to work. And I know it's early to be planning all that, but you know what I'm like. I do tend to be organised.'

'And I'm pretty sure Jenny will be all for that. But I can speak to her, or ask her to come and talk to you. Don't go letting that worry you. Concentrate on enjoying this very special time, won't you?' Callie grinned. 'I'm so happy for you both.'

'I'll try to enjoy it of course. Though I have to be honest — the quiche-cooking and the smell of baking pastry really are hard on my constitution, especially first thing in the morning. Haven't you seen me knocking back fizzy water and nibbling ginger biscuits like a crazy woman?'

Callie hadn't, but she was quick to jump in to find solutions to her friend's distress. 'Then how about we leave quiche prep for afternoons? Or better still, I can take over. I have to look after my staff, even if my own days here are numbered. You don't mind me packing it in, do you?'

'Of course,' Jonty kidded her. 'It's

completely selfish and I may never speak to you again.'

'Don't say that.' Callie grinned ruefully.

'Of course I don't mean it. I'm glad you're moving on and doing what you most want to. That's what's most important. Life will go on, even if I do miss you and pine for you like a puppy at a kennel. You're the best boss, you know that? I'm so going to miss you.'

'I'd hope so,' said Callie, feigning bravado. 'I'll miss you back more than you know. But I won't be a stranger just because I'm leaving the café. I'll be on hand for lunch during your maternity leave. And I might even work my way up to babysitting so you and Mack can get the odd night out at the cinema!'

'Cinema. Now there's a thought. I think I'd rather it was a four-course meal with all the trimmings. And wine! But it's going to be months yet until that can happen.'

'Well I can't wait to babysit, whenever it ends up happening. In fact I may even start knitting some little items now. We'll pick out some patterns together. I saw a book with these amazingly cute trendy animal hats.'

Jonty clasped her close. 'I knew I always loved you,' she said. And Callie had no doubt she meant it from the heart.

★   ★   ★

Hamish put his arm through Flora's as the breeze whipped his hair and filled his lungs. But even that couldn't whip away the strong and inextinguishable pain he felt. Every time he thought of Callie, he felt like somebody had singed his insides and twisted his emotions into a hard ball of barbed wire that stung him.

'I want to discuss the money I've left you, Hamish,' said Flora suddenly, taking him by surprise. 'I won't live forever . . .'

'Oh my goodness Aunty Flora. Stop right there!' Awkwardness and shock made Hamish stop in his tracks. He hadn't seen this coming. 'Neither of us are ready for this conversation.'

'Nevertheless, lad, it's one I want to have while I'm living. I'd've thought as a lawyer you'd respect that.'

He mumbled and cleared his throat. 'Sorry, Aunty. But you sure know how to shock a person.'

She nodded and walked again, patting his hand on her arm. 'You and your sister stand to inherit a substantial sum when I die. As you know, I own prime St. Andrews property — which I'm sure some golf-mad Yank or Japanese billionaire will be only too happy to snap up. And I have the house in the Highlands. You and Linley both stand to receive half — an equal share. However, I want you to have yours early. And to this end I'm selling up Bracken Cottage. You can have your share of the money now with my blessing — if you'll only stay here and say no to Europe.'

'But there's no need. I have a backer.

And I'm staying, whether Callie likes it or not.'

Flora watched him with wide eyes. 'You want to set up a law practice? I'd like to support you in that endeavour.'

'By the way,' Hamish added, 'that cottage double-booking thing. Completely underhand. Surprising for a woman of your years and refinement. Did you really think you'd get away with it?'

'A woman does what she has to do. Not that it worked as I'd hoped.' Flora clicked her tongue in disappointment. 'Anyway, half of my legacy is now entrusted to you. So what are your plans for this business start-up of yours?'

'Carter, my brother-in-law, has offered full backing for my plans. He's a great chap. He also believes in me as an investment, and we intend to take it further. Though I highly appreciate your support. So we don't need to be talking or thinking about inheritance or legacies yet. You've plenty of years in you, make no mistake.'

'And I am a lucky woman to have

you as a nephew. Did you know Callie has some health problem at the moment?'

Hamish stopped dead in his tracks on their walk through his aunt's garden. 'She's sick? What's wrong?' His heart was now racing madly and his mind doing somersaults to work out the quickest way to get to her.

'I heard through a friend that she's not been well, attending the doctor quite a few times. And she's seemed very low, as if something is pressing on her mind. I'm worried about her. Aren't you?'

'When it comes to Callie, I'm not sure what to think. We've got ourselves in a total mess. She doesn't even want to talk to me anymore.'

'There are things you need to understand about her, Hamish. Her father abandoned her to be raised by her grandparents. Jimmy Dewar was always a flaky sort, never stuck to much; and if he could blame somebody else and get away with it, he would.'

Hamish sighed deeply. 'Yes, yes . . .

sorry, Aunty, but can we do this another time? I had no idea Callie was sick. Didn't she explain more? What's your source? Are you really sure about this?' His mind was all over the issue. Did Callie have problems she'd kept from him? Now he thought about it, he was desperate to go and find her and get to the bottom of things.

His aunt tutted her frustration. 'She says not to worry, but she won't divulge details. What I'm trying to tell you, if you'll be patient enough to listen, is that Callie takes after her mother; her namesake. Carolina senior died of a stroke when Callie was tiny. Callie's Grandfather Angus took it hard because his son hardened as a result — he buried the sorrow and his anger in his work. Sound like somebody else we know? Her father shirked responsibility for another child he had. Jimmy only ever wanted money to fund his self-seeking ways. Callie finds it hard to put full trust in men, Hamish. Plain and simple.'

Hamish felt his heart clench for the

woman he loved. 'I knew her father disowned the business. Other details were sketchy. And now she's sick and I knew nothing about it.'

'She doesn't want to discuss it, not even with Linley, so I doubt she'll tell you.' Flora sucked in a breath. 'Her trust is shattered. She clings to that café because her grandfather was her world. She learned young not to trust, and developed a hard outer shell. And that brings me to my next point — she can't trust you'll stay. She thinks she's holding you back. You have to convince her.'

A penny dropped for Hamish. And it was a penny weighty in its implications. Callie wasn't rejecting him. She was sacrificing their relationship for some reason known only to her. She wanted him — she'd admitted as much — but something held her back. Was it to do with her illness? She'd already told him she doubted she'd have a family. Could that be the reason she was so hung up and reluctant to trust in him?

He felt his heart drum as he pulled his thoughts together. 'You're saying you think she imagines she's not enough for me? You're saying she has deep issues she can't get past?'

'Well, we can hardly blame her. We've spent a long time boasting about our brightest star, while Callie has been hiding all her feelings. Like the fact she's loved you for so long. There's much about Callie Dewar you've yet to find out.'

'Including what's been going on with her health. Now I'm crazy with worry.'

'I suggest you find her and make her understand she's all you need to make you happy. Once she grasps that essential fact — and it's something that's evaded her for her entire life — the rest may just find its own way home.'

'Her father was a flake. She lost her mother. She felt a duty to the café. She needs someone to put her first.'

'As much reassurance as you can give her and more. If you want to win her heart, convince her she can trust you and you won't leave her stranded.'

And he'd thought a whizz-bang diamond from an Edinburgh jeweller was the answer. He still wanted that ring on her finger, but first she had to see she was his only jewel. Her and her alone. Hamish hugged his fragile but tough-as-army-boots aunt and kissed her forehead tenderly.

'I love you, Aunt Flora. You're some woman. Fierce and fabulous. I'd never realised that I've never told Callie my job doesn't matter. My career's been great — but I want more than that. I want a home.'

'Tell your lassie what she needs to hear. And find out what this secret is that she's so distraught about. Nothing can't be beaten by love. For a clever man, you miss the obvious.'

He was a simpleton who'd forever love Callie Dewar to the moon and back again.

13

Callie had put extra logs on her burner, but the cold that had haunted her all day still iced her bones. A slouch night in pyjamas was what the doctor ordered after the day's events. She rarely ate junk food — a hangover from working with sweet treats all day — but tonight she'd hit the ice-cream bucket in a big way. And now the ice-cold chills had set in for good.

She used the poker to stoke the flames in the burner and grabbed a blanket. She even ignored the heavy knock at the door and shoved fists against her ears because she'd just got warmer and found the sofa's comfy spot. She didn't want to be caught like this — sad and dishevelled and pathetic.

'I'm not in, and I'm busy,' she shouted, knowing it made no sense.

'It's me, Jonty. Can I come in?'

Callie stifled a curse but went to the door, then rocked back on her heels to find Jonty walking away at speed to her car and leaving Hamish standing on the threshold. He wore inky jeans and his vintage leather jacket and boots.

She sucked in a gasp she didn't want to let out. 'It's as well I'm giving up the café or you'd be sacked,' she shouted after Jonty.

Hamish stared hard at her with one eyebrow raised.

'Isn't that a low trick, bringing a decoy to fool me on your behalf?'

'If it works, use it.'

'But then, I forgot — you'll go low to win the case.'

'I'll do whatever I need to when it comes to you, and I knew damn well you'd never let me in otherwise,' Hamish answered darkly. 'Can I come in? What's this about you being ill, Cal?'

'Do I have a choice about you coming in, or divulging anything?'

'Not when you have me uptight and

going crazy, no.' He moved to tower over her. 'What's happened?'

Callie brought him inside her barn conversion-turned fantasy home. But he stared only at her, not his surroundings. 'Well, then?' he said. 'Aren't you going to give me answers?'

'About my diagnosis — I don't need hospital or treatment or anything. It's a condition called premature ovarian failure. One that I just live with. It's not an outright no about the kids, but it's really low odds. So it's not life-threatening.'

Hamish let out a deep breath. 'Thank God for that.' Then he whistled softly, and she understood he hadn't expected what he now found in her unique home. 'You renovated this?' he asked, grey eyes wide and staring around him.

Callie nodded, her cheeks flushed at his interest. 'Me. And years of graft, saving, and make and mend. Most of it found for a song at auctions. I thought the derelict barn had potential as a space, but it was reduced to a wreck in a field. I had to live without a kitchen for two years — I still remember bathing in buckets, but it's okay now. In fact it makes my work at the café worth it.'

Hamish whistled again from between his teeth, taking in the high rafters, wooden gallery and artisan wood-crafted kitchen. 'Wow. Tell me about it.'

She watched him as he roved around. 'Created with love and hard work, plus the help of a local artisan eco-carpenter. Happily he loves cake, home-baked goodies and gourmet breads. His appetite is my gain.'

The stained-glass window featured a modern angel with vast wings. A panel of recycled glass bottles in shades from burgundy to green to cobalt graced the central wall.

Callie walked closer to the arresting pane. 'That wall is my favourite; I love it at sunset when the colours dance. Though the bathroom's pretty special; it has a wooden kayak bath.'

A driftwood and log mantelpiece fit

for a gothic cathedral in a glen was the showstopper, and she loved that Hamish had to reach out and touch things; she relished tactile reactions. When he spotted her ironwork mirror and gasped, she felt a kick of delight in her chest.

'Be in no doubt that people will buy your work,' he said. 'You're so much more than a cake-baker. You must go public with this. I'm humbled. And you're gifted.'

In the open dining area, metalwork chairs like fairy thrones conjured by a farrier graced the scene, along with a majestic wood table. Callie smiled as he gawped.

'I want that for myself.'

'Can't,' she laughed. 'Not for sale. Not yet, anyway.' She told him how the gallery upstairs led to more quirky features.

'This place is awesome, but it's not why I've come,' Hamish said. 'I want to stay here in St. Andrews and I want you in my life. No dreams of scaling legal heights other than my own practice, or maybe a university law teaching job. But more than that, I want you, Callie. Always have, always will — but you're too intent on pushing me out to see it.'

'You say that now, but what about when you get bored?' she whispered, the very thought making panic slice her lungs and squeeze her belly.

'I know that people have betrayed your trust. I recognise that you have low self-esteem — in fact, coming here and seeing all this glorious stuff that you're hiding away, unaware of your own talent, just underlines it. You have this crazy idea that we won't work. But we *will* work. We'll do more than that — we'll be sensational together. A bright, amazing future, because I couldn't love you any more than I already do.'

Callie paced away several steps, then returned and flicked a glance at the man she loved right back. 'It's not that simple. The diagnosis from my doctor alters things.' She had her fingers pressed to her mouth and she trembled slightly over the words. 'It means I can't be certain babies will happen for me. And that's something I'm finding hard to live with. I feel like my future's been blighted.'

Hamish walked to her and wrapped her in his embrace, not letting go. 'Oh Callie. You took all this on your own? Why haven't you asked for support? If not from me, from Linley? Because she and my aunt are nervous wrecks over you. As am I.'

'You can stop worrying, Hamish. It's not fatal. Just a blow that's knocked me emotionally in a very big way.'

'But you have people who love you. We all want to support you. Why not at least tell Linley?'

Callie's eyes filled with tears. 'She's only just back from honeymoon. I'm sure we all hope there'll soon be the patter of mini-golfing shoes in your family. I didn't want to darken any joy by dumping my woes on her.'

Hamish drew her to him, this time in a grip that claimed her as his own. 'And isn't that exactly why I love you to the moon and back?' She felt him study her face. 'You're so damn thoughtful, and yet you don't let us do the same for you. I have one more thing to ask — what happens if you do get pregnant? Is it dangerous?'

Callie shook her head. 'No. I have diminished chances of ever conceiving. Some women who have the condition do go on to have babies, but the odds are very much against it. Now do you see why I've tried to step away from us? It's for the best.'

She turned to search his gaze for clues, but he shrugged and felt in his pocket. He opened a ring box in his hand, revealing a diamond solitaire, and presented it to her. The sizeable gem glittered in its modern setting; it was the kind she'd have chosen herself, given the chance. Then he felt in his other pocket and drew out her mother's bracelet. It was fixed. How had he got it? Then Callie remembered leaving it with Agnes Drysdale, and she figured she'd been set up.

'You fixed it?' she said in a small voice.

- 'You broke my heart. I thought I should at least fix something. About the proposal — I've never been more serious. Marry me. Listen, if the answer's still no, I'm fine with not getting married. And I can withstand not having kids — though who's to say what the future will bring or that we wouldn't adopt some? Plenty of kids need a loving home like we'll have together if I have my way. I believe our relationship will work because I love you. And I've bought us a house in St. Andrews to prove that we'll have longevity and a future.' He gulped and took a breath. 'Trust me, Callie. My love is for real. It's the house you always admired with the glossy black door, Georgian sash windows and topiary trees. The one with the garden you go crazy about. I had a great chance to act quickly, so I did.'

'Hamish, you say that now . . . but what if you change your mind? And

311

what if we try for a family and it tears us apart? I couldn't bear to be your disappointment. It's too big a decision to make just like that.'

'I'm asking you again. Will you marry me?'

She stared into his grey eyes, trying to discern his true intent. Was this the ultimate in crazy sympathy? But before she could think further, he stopped her.

'This is me selfishly wanting you, Callie. Just you, because I love you and I want a future with you. So I don't care about tomorrow. Or next year. Or pregnancies that may or not be. This is just about us.'

She sucked in a gasp of pure blown-away bliss. 'After all I've done?'

'Because you're you. I can't help the fact I picked a woman who has spent half her life running in the opposite direction. Maybe it's living too close to the *Chariots of Fire* setting that's done it. You really love to run, Cal. But I also live to chase.'

She smiled, admiring that face she'd

yearned for so very long. Was it really true? God, she hoped so. 'I want to be chased by you, and only you, Hamish. I've loved you since I was a girl.'

He pulled her close to kiss her lips for stalled seconds of time. 'But you didn't answer my question. I want you to be my wife. I've never been more certain. What do you say?'

Inside, her heart sang and danced. She had craved this — being in his warm embrace and letting herself believe this moment was finally hers. 'Yes. I'm saying yes, I will marry you. I've said no for way too long. It's time to wake up to what I really want.'

Hamish swept her into his arms and kissed her until they were both drunk with the love they shared. When he eventually let go of her he whispered, 'Thank heavens for that. We've established you're a secret creative genius who only needs a push to rocket to the stars. And what's more, I love you, so I wouldn't give a jot if you were useless at everything you touched. It's you I want.

You and only you!' He circled her waist with his hands, then kissed her neck and nibbled a path to her chin-line. 'How come Linley never told me any of this?' he asked her. 'You need to talk to her about your health — she's thinking all the worst things, like I just did.'

'I will. I feel terrible for keeping her in the dark — I just hadn't processed the news enough myself. But I'll make amends soon. I think she may just forgive me when she takes a look at my ring finger!' Callie shook her head with remorse at her own thoughtlessness, but hugged her own growing sense of joy. She'd been so consumed in her own thoughts that she'd forgotten completely about other people's needs. She'd put that right, and vow to always do so.

'Tell Linley I'm sorry,' she said. 'I was in 'one day at a time' mode.'

'Enough about Linley. I love you and I want to marry you. And you said yes.'

Her heart skipped in her chest at the childlike look he gave her. 'Please sit down for a minute. There are things I need to explain.' She took in a long breath to fortify herself, then placed her hands on the table before her. 'I closed my heart up; sealed it over years ago. I'm not good with airing feelings. First Dad and his great disappearing act. Do you know I always felt like it was my fault he left?'

Hamish reached out to take her hand but he spoke no words, simply shaking his head.

'Then you and me all those years ago — the crush gone wrong. I wondered what I'd done. Had I turned you off?'

'I figured I was being a selfish clod stealing your heart and kisses, then going off to uni leaving you behind. I knew that if I suggested we go steady, you'd have used your integral role at the café as your reason not to come see me. So the intentions I thought were sound turned me into the idiot who abused your trust and hurt you all over again. Never think you're not enough, Callie. You're my every shade of wonderful. Your dad missed the good life he was so intent on chasing.'

Callie pulled herself against him, revelling in a brief hug because his words had hit deep. 'I got over it and put it behind me; focused on being what Gramps wanted me to be. But how could I ever realistically expect to be enough for you, the one who shot to success? And then you walk back into my life after I'd just had the worst news ever. Now do you see why I've tried to put distance between us?'

'But I'm nothing if not a fighter — and it's a trait that runs in my family.' Hamish smiled, then held her tight. 'Look at all this around you. I have no doubts you'll do amazingly in your next career. And anyway, I don't care about all that — it's you I want. You in pyjamas, or up a tree with a sheep ready to bite your ass. You and I together is all I'll ever need.'

Callie loved this man like no other. She loved him so hard all her life that she'd hardly dared wish for this moment to happen. Wishing had meant admitting it was the one thing — *he* was the one thing — she wanted above all else. And she'd always kept her dreams hidden, because hidden dreams couldn't be dashed.

'Nobody ever asked what *I* wanted, Hamish. Nobody ever cared enough. Nobody ever made me think I could be what I wanted. Obligation ran through the core of my family, and it slowly crushed me into a shell of who I used to be.'

'You're all that's important to me.' Hamish pulled her close and smoothed her hair against his chest. He smelled so divine that it knocked her back on her heels. Her breath caught as she relived the enormity of those words she'd never set free before. Injustice voiced. The burden eased enough for her to expel a long breath of relief. And suddenly a warm glow of burgeoning joy began to unfurl inside her that this was real and happening. Hamish loved her and knew her situation, and hadn't hesitated in pursuing his goal.

And oh how she wanted him now, with everything she had. He was opening her eyes up to what real, heart-felt love could offer. She should be similarly honest and true, she decided.

'I want you, too. Always have,' she admitted, reaching up and letting their mouths meet. She revelled in his kiss as their tongues danced to communicate need and desires reciprocated. 'I was so scared of wanting you that I ran. And I'm so sorry. I knew it was wrong, but I couldn't face my own fear.'

'It's not surprising you shut things out,' he told her. 'You've a right to feel angry.'

'I was most angry at my dad.'

'Rightly so, Cal. He was selfish.'

'I know. He didn't care about anything but himself, but I always thought it was somehow my fault. Getting the news that time might be limited to start my own family made that anger bubble up even more strongly. I'm sorry I was a nightmare to you in the café. I guess I took it out on you as the closest target!'

Hamish gave her a rueful grin. 'I'm man enough to take it. I knew you were in pain but had no idea why. I figured you had something against my profession or something.'

'My past left me disappointed, resigned to my fate and with self-esteem issues. I don't let my guard down easily. And I don't know if I'll ever have it in me to change. So as much as I want to want you — and God knows the kissing is an eye-opener — I honestly think I can't do this. Am I a lost cause?'

'Listen, Cal, sometimes we have to leave the past where it belongs. And having a family is not my first priority either. What right has anyone to plan the future? We have one past, a family. We could still try for babies; we'd have a damn great time on the way.' He sat blinking at her as a conclusion to his words. 'You don't have to feel alone. Linley cares, and I have your back now.'

Callie smiled slightly and his heart took flight. 'I want you right back. Can you handle helping me find out what I want?'

Hamish reached over, seizing her hands and searching her gaze. He bent to softly kiss each finger with precious care. 'Two can play at this 'find our future' game. And we can do it together.'

She had the man of her dreams pledging his love. She'd just got the lottery win. And to think she'd pushed him out harder than Dornoch had tried to dislodge her from the tree. Fortunately for her, Hamish hadn't ever given up hope. He was truly the man for her in every way, not least in fortitude and tenacity.

'I love you, Hamish.'

'As I do you.'

In seconds he had her in his arms. Before kissing her he told her, 'Count on me, Callie. Put your faith in our relationship and I'll prove to you we're worth it.'

'I do have one request,' she told him quietly, softly kissing his mouth.

'Name it. Anything.'

She took a deep breath, summoned courage, and went for her more heart-felt wish. 'I want us to try for a family as soon as we're married. No expectation. But we can try, can't we?' Okay, she did want to try a new career; she still wanted to sell the café. But some things were more pressing and far more important.

Her man's eyes shone. 'We certainly can,' he said with a grin. He palmed the back of his head, then grabbed her to kiss her again. 'We can hasten the wedding too. I don't want some big flash do, do you?'

'No. I've spent too much of my life waiting already.'

Hamish didn't have to be asked twice. He turned her in his arms and kissed her face, eyebrows, cheeks and eyelids. 'I can't live without you. I'm talking soon. A wedding in two months at the most.'

She laughed. 'I'm all for fast, but how about we compromise with 'by Christmas'? I still want to enjoy being a bride, with all the girlie stuff that goes with the job description. Even a fancy lawyer will have trouble stopping me from marrying you. I'm a force to be reckoned with when I get started.'

★   ★   ★

Bagpipe music swirled in the air, and outside in the grounds of Arrach Dean Craig a frosty white splendour lent a magical fairy-tale air to the Highland perfection backdrop. Everywhere Callie Dewar looked, kilted waiters in matching red-and-purple plaid hustled to and fro, serving their guests. Candles flickered, and the holly and ivy and red poinsettia theme vied with the towering Christmas tree for staging glory.

The dining room at Arrach Dean Craig was every bit as majestic and heart-stopping as Callie had dreamed it would be. How lucky was she to get this for her most special wedding day?

Jenny, her cousin, and Michael sat near to the expansive windows, and the looks they gave each other told Callie they'd be repeating their vows in similar surroundings soon themselves. Perhaps she'd throw her bouquet their way later. Much as she didn't want to part with the exquisite white Bianca rose hand-tied creation, she figured Jenny deserved the hint.

'Penny for your thoughts, Mrs. Gordon,' Hamish whispered near to her ear.

'I'm just thinking it's amazing what six months can achieve.'

St. Andrews was on the up and up. Callie recognised a few of the business association's faces around the room, and all of them looked both impressed and happy to come to her wedding. The hotel really was stunning now that it was open, and she felt proud to hand over the café's reins to someone way more passionate about its future success than she was. Gramps would have endorsed the move, she felt sure. Jenny had already reported that regularly she was fully booked, and the addition of the café to her business portfolio had proved a perfect combination. They'd both done the right thing.

'You mean you're thinking about something other than me?' Hamish teased. 'That's not allowed on your wedding day. Surely as your husband, I take priority.'

'Always the big head. You never change.'

He wore his full dress kilt, and she frankly couldn't wait for private time, a man in a kilt being utterly enticing. And most especially as they intended to try for children — with no guarantees; but why not? Miracle babies did happen, the doctor had told her. Ten percent of women with her condition did go on to manage to conceive. Whatever the outcome, she knew she was very blessed. She had the most beautiful Christmas wedding.

It had been an amazing half year of her life. Linley and Carter too had now confirmed their own happy baby news. Jonty's new arrival would be imminent. And a new year of opportunity lay ahead. The café was in safe, loving hands. And so was Callie.

As if summoned by her thoughts, a hand covered hers. 'I've already heard that people want to hire you for private interiors consultancy,' Hamish told her. 'They saw what you did to the rooms here. I think you may have a lot of work in your future. I'm hoping you'll say no and keep your focus on me.'

Callie smiled at her man. 'And here was me planning for some relaxation time now the café isn't mine. I think I'm going to have to be selective. But I do want to dabble.'

'Let's concentrate on us, Cal. That's the only project that gets our full attention for the foreseeable future. Let's see what that brings.' Hamish drew his wife to him and pressed his mouth over hers. 'I love you, Callie Dewar.'

'Love you right back, Mr. Gordon. Now that I've given up catering, I've developed a hankering for gold jewellery. Must've been the influence of this place. Gold fever.' She flashed her wedding band and a gratified grin before kissing Hamish again. 'We're going to be busy soon. New house. And have I told you how much I love the photographs displayed here? It may only be a hobby sideline, but your photography looks fantastic! Clever man of mine.'

Ginny winked at them, holding her bubbly six-month-old to her; he was dressed up in his tiny first kilt. 'You two look cosy.'

'We are. Makes you sick, eh?' Hamish replied. 'We'll be using disgusting pet names next. And you look like a woman who's in love with another man.' Hamish winked at her and gently cooed to Ginny and Cam's young son.

'I only have eyes for my main man. My PookieBun will always be special — even if he still drives me crazy. He's promising to do some step-dancing to entertain everyone later. Please save us from that. You like the venue?'

Callie hugged her friend and baby both. 'How could anyone not love this? Princess for a day. The perfect wedding gift. I can never thank you enough.'

'And what a princess you are in that dress,' Ginny said, beaming. 'In fact, I think your wedding has gone down very well indeed. Even the seniors approve.'

They watched the small group at fireside. Eyes twinkling, Flora and her friends Agnes and Alec toasted them with their favourite whisky from the bar beside the crackling fireplace. Flora wore a symphony of tartan with a tall feather and glimmering brooch in her hat, while Alec wore a full dress kilt to match his wife's tartan sash.

'Aren't they sweet together?' Agnes commented to Flora. 'Your plan worked a treat.'

'Shame we had to pick up a thieving criminal pitfall on the way, but we got there in the end, didn't we?'

'Conniving women,' said Alec. 'The witches of *Macbeth* have nothing on you two.'

'Slainte Vhar!' they chorused.

'Slainte Vhar,' answered Callie, clinking her flute glass.

'Slainte Vhar,' Hamish whispered,

softly kissing his wife. 'You see, as we've told you, my family has a bad habit of getting our way in the end. It's in the Gordon genes, in case you hadn't already guessed.'

Other titles in the
Linford Romance Library:

SECRETS OF MELLIN COVE

Rena George

After Wenna discovers a shocking family secret, she flies to the comfort of her beloved Cornish moors. What can she do? If she reveals the terrible truth, her family will be ruined. If she does nothing, she could be condemning the crew of a sailing ship to death. Perhaps she should confide in the tall stranger who rides past her every day, always casting an interested glance in her direction. But would he understand, or would he go straight to the authorities? No, she couldn't trust a stranger . . . or could she?